BLOWN SKY-HIGH

Touch the Sky heard the tiny sound of metal clinking and glanced straight up into the dazzling sunlight. It was impossible to see much more than a vague human shape suddenly duck out of sight. But that split-second warning was enough to prime Touch the Sky to danger when something heavy bounced off the rawhide shield strapped to his rope rigging.

The object bounced high enough for the brave to suddenly snake one hand out to catch it. He had never before seen the new grenades close-up. But thanks to his schooling among the whites, he was able to read just enough letters of the word explosive. Instead of gripping the object, he struck it as hard as he could with his palm, swatting it over into a pile of scree.

A heartbeat later, an earsplitting detonation shook the ground....

CHEYENNE

15

RENEGADE NATION

JUDD COLE

LEISURE BOOKS **NEW YORK CITY**

A LEISURE BOOK®

December 1995

Published by

Dorchester Publishing Co., Inc.
276 Fifth Avenue
New York, NY 10001

Prologue

Although Matthew Hanchon bore the name given to him by his adopted white parents, he was the son of full-blooded Northern Cheyennes. The lone survivor of a Bluecoat massacre in 1840, the infant was raised by John and Sarah Hanchon in the Wyoming Territory settlement of Bighorn Falls.

His parents loved him as their own, and at first the youth was happy enough in his limited world. The occasional stares and threats from others meant little—until his sixteenth year and a forbidden love with Kristen, daughter of the wealthy rancher Hiram Steele.

Steele's campaign to run Matthew off like a distempered wolf was assisted by Seth Carlson, the jealous, Indian-hating cavalry officer who was in love with Kristen. Carlson delivered a fateful ultimatum: Either Matthew cleared out of Bighorn

5

Falls for good, or Carlson would ruin his parents' contract to supply nearby Fort Bates—and thus, ruin their mercantile business.

His heart sad but determined, Matthew set out for the upcountry of the Powder River, Cheyenne territory. Captured by braves from Chief Yellow Bear's tribe, he was declared an Indian spy for the hair-face soldiers. He was brutally tortured over fire. But only a heartbeat before he was to be scalped and gutted, old Arrow Keeper interceded.

The tribe shaman and protector of the sacred Medicine Arrows, Arrow Keeper had recently experienced an epic vision. This vision foretold that the long-lost son of a great Cheyenne chief would return to his people—and that he would lead them in one last, great victory against their enemies. This youth would be known by the distinctive mark of the warrior, the same birthmark Arrow Keeper spotted buried past this youth's hairline: a mulberry-colored arrowhead.

Arrow Keeper used his influence to spare the youth's life. He also ordered that he be allowed to join the tribe, training with the junior warriors. This infuriated two braves especially: the fierce war leader, Black Elk, and his cunning younger cousin, Wolf Who Hunts Smiling.

Black Elk was jealous of the glances cast at the tall young stranger by Honey Eater, daughter of Chief Yellow Bear. And Wolf Who Hunts Smiling, proudly ambitious despite his youth, hated all whites without exception. This stranger, to him, was only a make-believe Cheyenne who wore white man's shoes, spoke the paleface tongue, and showed his emotions in his face like the woman-hearted white men.

Arrow Keeper buried his white name forever and gave him a new Cheyenne name: Touch the Sky. But he remained a white man's dog in the eyes of many in the tribe. At first humiliated at every turn, eventually the determined youth mastered the warrior arts. Slowly, as his coup stick filled with enemy scalps, he won the respect of more and more in the tribe.

He helped save his village from Pawnee attack; he defeated ruthless whiskey traders bent on destroying the Indian way of life; he outwitted land-grabbers intent on stealing the Cheyenne homelands for a wagon road; he saved Cheyenne prisoners kidnapped by Kiowas and Comanches during a buffalo hunt; he rode north into the Bear Paw Mountains to save Chief Shoots Left Handed's Cheyennes from Seth Carlson's Indian-fighting regiment; he ascended fearsome Wendigo Mountain to recover the stolen Medicine Arrows; and he saved Honey Eater and many others when he risked his life to obtain vaccine against deadly Mountain Fever.

But with each victory, deceiving appearances triumphed over reality, and the acceptance he so desperately craved eluded him. Worse, his hard-won victories left him with two especially fierce enemies outside the tribe: a Blackfoot called Sis-ki-dee and a Comanche named Big Tree.

As for Black Elk, at first he was hard but fair. When Touch the Sky rode off to save his white parents from outlaws, Honey Eater was convinced that he had deserted her and the tribe forever. She was forced to accept Black Elk's bride-price after her father crossed to the Land of Ghosts. But Touch the Sky returned.

Then, as it became clear to all that Honey Eater loved Touch the Sky only, Black Elk's jealousy drove him to join his younger cousin in plotting against Touch the Sky's life. Finally, Wolf who Hunts Smiling's treachery forced a crisis: Aiming at Touch the Sky in heavy fog, he instead killed Black Elk. Now Touch the Sky stands accused of the murder in the eyes of many.

Though it divided the tribe irrevocably, he and Honey Eater performed the squaw-taking ceremony. He has firm allies in his blood brother Little Horse, the youth Two Twists, and Tangle Hair. With Arrow Keeper's mysterious disappearance, Touch the Sky is the tribe shaman. But a pretend shaman named Medicine Flute, backed by Touch the Sky's enemies, has challenged his authority. And despite his fervent need to stop being the eternal outsider, Touch the Sky is still trapped between two worlds, welcome in neither.

Chapter One

"Fathers and brothers, have ears for my words!" Wolf Who Hunts Smiling exhorted those assembled in the council lodge. "They are words you may place in your sashes and take away with you, words worthy of careful examination. I say it now, and this place hears me. This council is tainted because *that* one has the putrid stink of the murderer on him!"

Touch the Sky held his face impassive as every brave in the lodge, ranging from young, unblooded warriors to the hoary-haired clan Headmen, stared where Wolf Who Hunts Smiling pointed—directly at the only man among them who had been raised by whites.

Everyone waited for Touch the Sky to respond. Still revealing no emotion in his face, the youth called out to a sturdy little warrior sitting near the center pole. "Little Horse! Have you noticed a thing?"

Little Horse, quickly responding to the devil-may-care tone of his friend's voice, replied in the same tone. "What thing is this, brother?"

"Although we are well into the Moon When the Geese Return, it is still so cold in the mornings that one can see his pony's piss steam."

"Indeed, I have noticed this very thing."

"And yet, the days quickly grow warm, for just now when this wolf opened his mouth, the dung that fell from it gave off no steam."

A few younger braves, caught by surprise, laughed. Most of them were members of the Bow String soldier society who were loyal to Touch the Sky. No one had expected such brazen effrontery. This was a formal Council of Forty, convened to discuss the thorny issue of selecting a new war leader to replace the dead Black Elk. Yet Touch the Sky had not even bothered to rise when he spoke—a clear insult to Wolf Who Hunts Smiling.

This enraged brave now turned to face a silver-haired warrior who presided from the middle of the lodge. "Gray Thunder, you have eyes to see and ears to hear! You know me. My lips have touched the common pipe after yours have smoked it. And those lips now swear by the four directions that this one, who mocks the dignity of this council, murdered my cousin in order to marry his squaw!"

"Odd," Chief Gray Thunder replied calmly, "that you can swear by the four directions to know this thing. For truly, no one else in this camp knows it so surely."

"The pistol that killed my cousin was discovered in his tipi!"

"Yes," Little Horse said, "and that pistol was stolen from a Sioux whose tipi you often visited, wily wolf."

"I have no ears for these lies! If I—"

"*I* am the one who has no ears," Gray Thunder cut in. "We did not meet here to rake through old coals. The purpose of this council is to vote with the stones and select our next war leader."

Gray Thunder was a respected peace leader. Touch the Sky knew that this pronouncement should have settled the matter. But now he watched a furtive glance pass between Wolf Who Hunts Smiling and Lone Bear, leader of the Bull Whip soldier society. Lone Bear rose to speak.

"Fathers and brothers! Gray Thunder is our chief, and no man here can say we chose a bad one. But count my coup feathers! I am a soldier troop leader, and I say, only think on this thing. Because he died unclean, with no chance to sing his death song, we can never again pronounce the name of him who is no longer with us. Yet was he not a warrior to be reckoned with? How many times did he rout Pawnees from breastworks and count coup on the Crow Crazy Dogs? How many times did his valor and fighting fettle save this tribe from destruction?

"And yet, only think. Who has been punished for his cold-blooded murder? There is no crime worse, to an honorable Cheyenne, than the murder of a fellow tribesman! All of you know that the murder stink never washes off, either from the tribe or from the murderer. Wolf Who Hunts

11

Smiling spoke straight-arrow: This council is tainted, for there must be a murderer among us!"

Lone Bear, too, stared at Touch the Sky with eyes that reflected bitter hatred. Knowing that conciliation and cooperation had long ago become impossible, Touch the Sky only stared coldly back. A strong, hawk nose was set between keen black eyes and a mouth that formed a straight, determined slit under pressure. Normally he wore his long black hair in loose locks, cut short over his brow to free his vision. But in honor of the council he had braided it and wrapped the single braid in strips of red-painted buckskin.

Only a fool, Touch the Sky told himself, could not see how things stood: This was a tribe divided against itself and teetering on the brink of inner-tribal war.

"Not only are we tainted by this murderer among us," spoke up a skinny youth named Medicine Flute in his odd, high-pitched voice. "But he now keeps our Sacred Arrows and tops the widow of the man he murdered."

Despite Medicine Flute's unmanly appearance and indifference toward the warrior arts, Touch the Sky knew he was adept at faking trances and visions. Thus, abetted by his chief supporter, Wolf Who Hunts Smiling, he had risen in prestige to the point where he now openly challenged Touch the Sky for the title of tribe shaman.

But at his last words, Touch the Sky felt warm blood creep into his face. Now he did indeed stand up. And when he did, so did the warriors named Little Horse, Tangle Hair, and Two Twists.

"Do not mention my wife one more time, bone

blower," Touch the Sky told him. This was an allusion to the hollowed-out leg-bone instrument that Medicine Flute constantly played. "If you ever say her name in my hearing, I will cut out your tongue and feed it to the camp dogs while you watch."

Rage turned Medicine Flute's face livid, but fear held him in check. "All in good time," he said mysteriously, locking glances with Wolf Who Hunts Smiling. "The worm will turn, and soon."

However, he said no more. The four braves now standing, hands resting on the sheaths of their knives, sat behind few men in council despite their relative youth. And it was common knowledge that any buck who tried to kill Touch the Sky must kill all of them. Even so, the defiant rage in Wolf Who Hunts Smiling's furtive, swift-as-minnow eyes showed no fear, for he was one born to command—the need for power burned inside him like hell thirst. Now he spoke.

"You may play the big Indian and threaten Medicine Flute, but you cannot throw the attention off your own treachery! You are a spy for the hair-faced soldiers! I call you White Man Runs Him! You have cleverly beguiled our former shaman and certain other doting old elders who are in their frosted years. You have convinced them you have the gift of visions.

"But the foulest dogs always return to their own vomit. The cowardly murder of my cousin has made even your staunchest supporters take a closer look. Soon your disloyalty to the *Shaiyena* way will once again be out for all to see."

Touch the Sky was not fooled by all this smoke.

13

Wolf Who Hunts Smiling had no more concern for his dead cousin than he had for a handful of spider leavings. Indeed, Touch the Sky was convinced that he had killed his own cousin, albeit unintentionally.

No—the hot-headed young buck had a far greater grievance against Touch the Sky. He had once bribed an old grandmother into claiming she'd had a 'vision' about Touch the Sky—one that said he must undergo a terrible penance or the entire tribe was lost. The Cheyenne faith in vision claims was powerful. Consequently, Touch the Sky had "swung from the pole"—curved bone hooks were driven into his breasts and he was suspended from them for hours, fierce red waves of pain washing over him. But the old shaman, Arrow Keeper, eventually exposed Wolf Who Hunts Smiling's treachery. The Council of Forty had voted to strip the errant buck of his coup feathers—a devastating blow to this proud warrior, who still could not display his battle record for all to see.

"Hold," interceded Chief Gray Thunder when Touch the Sky was about to reply. "I command silence from both of you! I only tolerated you two so long to make the point clear—our tribe is in a dangerous way. For truly, though it pains me to admit it, everyone present knows there are two braves equally qualified to serve as battle leader. And those two braves, even now, are at each other's throat."

Gray Thunder paused. For a long moment nothing could be heard but the bent-sapling frame of the lodge creaking in a sudden breeze.

"Things are the way they are," Gray Thunder resumed. "I would do much to alter them if it lay in my power. It is not the way of a Cheyenne chief to dictate to his people. Rather, he is the voice of the people, expressing their common will. However, recent events have forced me to extraordinary measures to protect my people."

He glanced first at Wolf Who Hunts Smiling, then at Touch the Sky, his face stern. "Know this. A vote now with the stones might well end in bloodshed. I have gone to the Star Chamber in secret. And in secret they have selected our next battle leader. He will serve until events in this village again permit a peaceful vote."

This astounded most of those present, although Touch the Sky welcomed the news. For he, too, saw bloodshed ahead if this thing came to a vote. The Star Chamber was the Cheyenne court of last resort. Made up of secret members known only to Chief Gray Thunder, their word was final and could not be questioned.

All eyes stared at the chief, curious. "Our new war chief," he announced, "will be Spotted Tail, leader of the Bow String troop."

Relief swept through Touch the Sky and his friends. But immediately Wolf Who Hunts Smiling, Medicine Flute, Lone Bear, and many others were on their feet.

"Foul!" shouted Wolf Who Hunts Smiling. "Spotted Tail has already publicly sworn his loyalty to Touch the Sky."

"And repeats it now," Spotted Tail spoke out boldly.

"Yes, to regret it later," Touch the Sky heard Medicine Flute mutter.

"As I said," Gray Thunder repeated firmly, "things are the way they are. Spotted Tail is our battle chief. The Star Chamber has spoken. You two"—here he again shared a disapproving stare between Wolf Who Hunts Smiling and Touch the Sky—"have got this tribe devouring its own tail. Until some real peace is established between you, Spotted Tail remains battle chief."

Touch the Sky spoke out first, and it was his words that ended the council.

"Father, have ears! The only peace possible between me and Wolf Who Hunts Smiling is the eternal peace of death. We two will clash, and one of us will die. He has conspired with enemies of this tribe, and his treachery has cost the blood of our own. Further, in my heart of hearts, I am convinced it was he who murdered our war leader, intending the bullet for me. No, there is no peace possible. And know that his blood will not stain the sacred Arrows, for he is not a true Cheyenne."

It bothered Touch the Sky when the fiery-tempered Wolf Who Hunts Smiling let this pass without comment. But it bothered him even more when he saw the sly smile his enemy exchanged with Medicine Flute.

No doubt about it. Once again, Touch the Sky told himself, his enemies had treachery firmly by the tail.

The highest peak in the Sans Arc Mountains was known to all local Indians as Wendigo Mountain. It was located a full sleep's ride from Gray Thunder's summer camp at the confluence of the Powder and Little Powder Rivers, and its craggy summit was the most taboo place on the Great Plains. To subdue her spiteful children, a Cheyenne mother only need promise, "If you're not good, I'll send you to Wendigo Mountain!"

The cause of such bad medicine was rooted, not in Cheyenne lore, but in true tribal history as recorded by the annual winter-count maintained in pictographs by the elders. It happened during the darkest days of the *Shaiyena* people, after Pawnees managed to capture the sacred Medicine Arrows. A group of Cheyenne hunters was trapped out on the prairie by a huge Crow war party—and Crow Crazy Dogs, at that.

The Crazy Dogs were the highly feared suicide warriors: once engaged in battle, they were sworn either to defeat their enemies or to die to the last man. The Cheyennes fled into the Sans Arc range. They selected the peak now known as Wendigo Mountain because it was the most formidable. Because of its constant mists, caused by underground steam leaks trapped in the high winds, they did not realize the opposite slope was in fact nothing but sheer cliffs.

The relentless and fanatical Crazy Dogs locked onto their quarry like hounds on a blood scent. They backed the Cheyennes on to the cliffs, where the defenders soon depleted all their musket balls and arrows. Rather than give the Crazy Dogs the pleasure of torturing them, the Cheyennes all sang their death song. As one, all twelve hunters linked arms and stepped off the cliffs and were impaled on the basalt turrets far below. Their bodies were never recovered.

They died unnatural deaths after dark. Bad deaths that left them in eternal torment, doomed—according to the legend that now took over from history—to haunt Wendigo Mountain. Still today, swore many Indians, you could hear their groans in the moaning of the wind.

And it was here, in the most unholy of places, that Wolf Who Hunts Smiling had chosen to establish his new Renegade Nation.

He sat his pure black pony, flanked by Medicine Flute on one side and the loyal, if dim-witted, Swift Canoe on the other. Two more riders had just joined them—two riders who commanded attention and yet defied eye contact. For truly, Wolf Who Hunts Smiling told himself, no other renegades between the Pecos and the Marias were the equal of the north-country Blackfoot warrior called Sis-ki-dee and the Comanche terror from the Southwestern plains, Big Tree.

"Greetings, wily Wolf Who Hunts Smiling!" Sis-ki-dee called out, raising his North & Savage rifle high to show it was still in its buckskin sheath and thus no threat. He spoke the familiar mix of Sioux and Cheyenne words understood by most Plains tribes. "Will you count coup on me again as you did when first we met?"

His famous lupine grin split Wolf Who Hunts Smiling's normally expressionless face. "I was wise to do so, Contrary Warrior. For thus I impressed you and left you curious enough to hear my plan."

"That plan failed, wily wolf. But it was a good

18

one. And thus, like our Comanche friend here, I have come at the time you requested, all to hear this new one. For also like the two of you, I will sleep much better after this tall shaman has been sent to his scaffold."

Big Tree laughed outright as he dismounted from the right side—the Indian side—of his ginger mustang. "You two jays! Listen to this idle chatter. You speak about killing *that* one so casually, as if you were selecting a buffalo from the herd? I have heard peyote soldiers talk thus."

Sis-ki-dee took no offense at this, only grinning as he watched the huge Comanche hobble his pony's foreleg to the rear with rawhide. Brass rings dangled from the slits in Sis-ki-dee's ears, and heavy copper brassards protected his upper arms from enemy lances and arrows. His face was badly marred by smallpox scars. In defiance of the long-haired Blackfoot tribe that had banished him forever, he and all of his contrary braves wore their hair cropped ragged and short.

"You do well to remind us about the Bear Caller," Sis-ki-dee admitted to Big Tree. "We have gloated before, only to end up doing the hurt dance."

"Who knows this better than I?" Wolf Who Hunts Smiling challenged them. "Which of you has lived in the same tribe with him as I have been forced to do? Which of you has lost his coup feathers because the cowardly old elders, now too weak to rut or fight, take his side against me?"

"Would you cry like a woman?" Big Tree said, his voice dripping scorn. "Coup feathers! You Cheyenne are just like your Sioux cousins. Let someone announce that they have rutted on your mother, and you are ready to fall on your knife to regain your honor. All this scalp-curing and whacking ponies on the rump with your silly sticks! We Comanches want women and gold, good tobacco, prisoners to ransom to the Comancheros. Useful things. You Cheyennes are worthy enough fighters, so you have three sleeps to paint and dance and put the trance glaze on. We Comanches are ready to kill in an eyeblink."

Sis-ki-dee enjoyed this and again laughed his insane laugh. He had heard of the Comanche trick rider Big Tree, but never seen this fearsome red raider up close before. It was said he rode a crow-hopping horse as easily as most good men could sit on the ground, that at a full gallop he could string and shoot twenty arrows in the time it took a Bluecoat pony soldier to load and fire his carbine once.

Big Tree, in turn, gazed back at the Blackfoot legend with evident respect. For everyone knew that the insane Contrary Warrior had been born at the very same moment when a wild-eyed black stallion raced past the tipi. And true to this awful omen, he had grown up wild-eyed and crazy dangerous. Big Tree could see clearly now that this one was incapable of fear—no wonder there was a generous bounty on his head up in the Bear Paw country of Montana, where he had once led a reign of terror over red and white men alike.

Wolf Who Hunts Smiling was still chafing at Big Tree's insults. But he held his anger in check, realizing what was at stake here.

"You speak straight words," he assured Big

Tree. "The Indians who survive the invasion by the *Mah-eesh-ta-shee-da* must be ready killers. In this, the northern warriors need lessons from the Comanche. That is why you will be so important to this new nation, Big Tree. For you will be our war leader and train all the young bucks in the true art of killing."

"New nation? Are we girls in our sewing lodges, playing make-believe places? Talk plain words like a man and leave these riddles to shamen."

Again Big Tree's arrogant tone irritated Wolf Who Hunts Smiling. But indeed, Big Tree had spoken as he himself might have. He was a man who knew piss from rain.

"Well then, bucks," Wolf Who Hunts Smiling said, "are these words plain enough? I want you to bring your bands together here, right here on Wendigo Mountain. Permanently. For in time I, too, will bring my band to join with yours. And then the three of us will rule over an impregnable new Renegade Nation that will play havoc on red and white foes alike."

At first his two visitors only gaped stupidly, wondering if this Cheyenne had been struck by lightning. But very quickly, Sis-ki-dee lost his look of wonder as he glanced around them. Once before he himself had chosen this spot for a defensive bastion. Wendigo Mountain was steep and virtually unscalable. It had been scoured by wind and rain for millennia until it was worn down to sheer cliffs except for one narrow, talus-strewn approach. The same approach he had taken to arrive at this spot.

Big Tree, too, had slowly altered his thinking as

he saw the Blackfoot gazing about them. "Let us suppose, Cheyenne, that your new Renegade Nation was a plan worth loading a pipe over, worth turning over so we may examine it further. What about the tall shaman? Nothing has worked against him before. My men are safe in the Blanco Canyon country, they are used to it. Before I bring them to this cold land, I would need many assurances. And chief among them must be your assurance that the tall shaman dies."

"My men are already near this place," Sis-ki-dee conceded. "But never forget: Once before they camped here. And the tall Bear Caller routed them from this place with fear-spittle dripping from their lips. Only the promise of great riches could lure my warriors back to this place. And I cross my lance over Big Tree's on this other point: I will not bring my men here unless you have a sure plan for destroying this tall one."

"Riches?" Wolf Who Hunts Smiling threw his head back and laughed, the sound almost drowned out in a howling gust of wind. "Who will stop us from plundering this land and all who pass through it? For I assure you—as surely as I have breath in my nostrils, White Man Runs Him will soon have none in his!"

"Idle boasting," scoffed Big Tree. "Both on the matter of riches *and* killing our enemy."

"Not at all," Wolf Who Hunts Smiling assured him. "Sis-ki-dee, you know of Caleb Riley's gold mine close to this place?"

"How could I not, you fool? It cost me twenty braves trying to take it."

"It won't cost you five this next time."

The crazy glint in Sis-ki-dee's eyes intensified. "No? And how can our wily wolf be so smug?"

"Because," the Cheyenne answered confidently, "I will help you attack it while Touch the Sky is down in Bighorn Falls, defending his white parents from Big Tree here."

Another long silence while the fierce winds of Wendigo Mountain howled and shrieked all about them, sounding very much indeed like souls in pain. Abruptly, the Comanche met the Blackfoot's eye and both men nodded simultaneously. Sly smiles creased their faces.

Wolf Who Hunts Smiling watched this and nodded his approval. "Come," he said, "let us build a fire and load a pipe while I convince you that *this* time our fish is gut-hooked."

Chapter Two

Touch the Sky tossed in a fitful sleep while images from his troubled past stampeded through his mind.

He was Matthew Hanchon again, not Touch the Sky. He glimpsed the unshaven, long-jawed face of Hiram Steele's wrangler Boone Wilson, again saw him unsheathing his Bowie knife while Steele's daughter Kristen screamed. He flexed another memory muscle, and now he saw the smug, overbearing sneer of Seth Carlson, the bluecoat lieutenant who had helped Steele try to destroy John and Sarah Hanchon's mercantile business.

There was more, images flying past like quick geese in a windstorm. He saw his own people tormenting him over fire as a spy, the only crime for which Cheyenne law demanded torture. He saw the whiskey traders again slaughtering white trappers and making the killings look "Indian," saw himself counting coup on Seth Carlson when the officer tried to torch the Hanchon spread. Again, in the vivid paintings of his dream, he saw the terrified Pawnees fleeing from Medicine Lake when he summoned a ferocious grizzly. Once more the keelboat called the *Sioux Princess* exploded into splinters as he led his people to victory over the land-grabber Wes Munro during the now-famous Tongue River Battle.

All these images and many more, the most harrowing of all being also the most recent: the image of Black Elk lying dead on the ground, killed by a coward's shot to the back of his head. Only moments before, in the finest gesture of his stormy life, Black Elk had made a peace of sorts with Touch the Sky. And then he was struck down before he could sing his death song.

But a shaman's dream never unleashed old images for no purpose. Mixed in with all the fragments from his past were glimpses from his vision-quest at Medicine Lake, glances stolen from the future: He saw his people freezing far to the north in the Land of the Grandmother, saw Cheyenne blood staining the snow. The screams of the dying ponies were even more hideous than the death cries of the Cheyenne.

It all led to one huge battle. And then the warrior leading the entire Cheyenne Nation in its last great stand turned to utter the war cry, and Touch the Sky recognized the face under the long war bonnet as himself.

Outside the fitfully tossing brave and past the edge of the still camp, wind whipped up the cottonwood leaves and set them rustling. Out of this rising noise, Arrow Keeper's voice suddenly spoke to him.

Soon, once again, little brother, you must remember Chief Yellow Bear's advice: When all seems lost, become your enemy! For the battles now coming, red man's magic will guard one flank, white man's cunning the other. Count equally on each of them and the battle is yours to win. But neglect either, and you lose all!

"Touch the Sky? Touch the Sky! Wake up, husband, it is only a dream."

His eyes eased open, still blurry with the cobwebs of sleep. He blinked them clear, and then a smile slowly melted the grim set of his lips.

"Only a dream," Honey Eater repeated soothingly. "And a bad one, clearly."

"Only one cure for bad dreams," he assured her.

"Oh? This is shaman's lore you never taught me."

"No," he corrected her. "It is white man's custom, and I did indeed teach it to you. Though truly, you were an apt pupil and soon became the teacher."

She blushed at this, but gave the truth to his words by bending further forward to kiss his lips. For indeed, red men did not kiss their women. But when Touch the Sky first kissed her, long before her father, Yellow Bear, crossed over, it had made her smile inside as nothing else could.

"Look at you," he said, brushing her hair with his lips. "Sister Sun only now peeking from her bed, yet you have gathered flowers already."

His lips brushed one of the fresh, fragrant white

columbine petals she had braided into her hair. One hand traced the delicate sculpting of her high cheek bones. It was thus he discovered the warm tears in the corners of her eyes.

He cupped her chin and turned her evasive face toward his. "What?" he said simply, knowing that she was not one to hold back from him.

"What? Only that you looked so handsome lying there asleep! So handsome—and so troubled! Touch the Sky, everyone in this village sings your praises as a warrior. And well they might, Cheyenne, for none braver lives outside of legend. I only wish—I only—"

Sobs suddenly escaped like tight bubbles rising from her. Touch the Sky did not push for more words now, but only held her. And as he knew it would, the real reason of her tears now revealed itself.

"I only wish," she continued bravely, "that I could give you a child, as a wife should. Yet, soon, once again, I must go to the once-a-month lodge."

She was telling him, Touch the Sky realized, that her bleeding time had come.

"Why cry," Touch the Sky said calmly, "over decisions made by Maiyun? We will have our child when the time is best for it. If not, I was luckier than ten braves when you lay your robes beside mine."

These words, and his tone, did much to calm her. Yet, one grief aside, she again thought of his tormented face just now as he lay sleeping. While Honey Eater watched, Touch the Sky rose up on one elbow and picked up the bride-gift she had presented him at their squaw-taking: a beautiful necklace made from the foreclaws of a grizzly. He studied it thoughtfully.

"Our marriage," she said, "has turned this tribe into two enemy camps."

"No. Wolf Who Hunts Smiling and his pack of fawning dogs have done that. Our marriage was only the lightning bolt that clearly scored the tree."

"Of course, it is as you say. Before he crossed, my father"—here Honey Eater quickly made the cut-off sign, as one did when speaking of the dead—"told me about the time Wolf Who Hunts Smiling walked between you and the campfire. Thus he announced his intention to kill you some day. He is no man of honor, but one vow he always keeps is his promise to kill."

Touch the Sky listened to all this. But as he did so, he continued to thoughtfully study the necklace.

"Husband?"

"Yes?" Lost in thought, Touch the Sky did not realize he had spoken in English.

"Why are you so absorbed in that necklace?"

He glanced up, startled. "Am I? Perhaps I am only chasing a will-o'-the wisp. But it almost seems as if . . . as if I have been dreaming more lately since leaving this beside our robes when we sleep."

At these words, Honey Eater's close attention transformed itself into obvious apprehension. Now it was Touch the Sky's turn to be curious. "Why do you ask me this thing?" he demanded.

"I will tell you, but do not laugh at me."

"If you make me promise, young sprite, then I

will try not to laugh. But I confess, I do not feel a jest is coming from you."

"None. Only this. I made that necklace because Arrow Keeper appeared to me in a dream and ordered me to do so."

Indeed, humor was the last thing these words inspired in Touch the Sky. Everything he knew of the shamanic arts had been learned from Arrow Keeper.

"I do not claim it was a medicine dream," Honey Eater said apologetically.

"Any dream with Arrow Keeper in it is a medicine dream," Touch the Sky assured her, again studying the necklace twined around his fingers. "Long ago Arrow Keeper taught me that the claws of the grizzly are powerful medicine."

The fear in Honey Eater's eyes silenced Touch the Sky before he spoke his final sentence: *And he sent them to me because of this new battle coming.* Red man's magic on one flank, white man's cunning on the other, he reminded himself.

But what did it mean: *Neglect either one, and you lose all?*

Sis-ki-dee rode a newly broken roan pony with a white belly, called a sabino by the Southwest halfbreed from whom he had stolen her. Though young, the mare was bridle wise: she would instantly change directions once the reins were laid on the side of her neck. She was also trained to halt instantly if the reins touched the ground.

Sis-ki-dee dropped them now, stopping his mount behind a huge pile of glacial moraine. The number of Crooked Feet (as Sis-ki-dee called

29

white men because their toes slewed outward when they walked) below surprised him into a deep frown. Indeed, in his absence this had become more of a town than a mining camp.

Caleb Riley's Far West Mining Company had built its headquarters camp in the Sans Arc range, nearly one full sleep's ride to the northwest of the Powder River Cheyenne camp. It was located in a teacup-shaped hollow about halfway up a mountain that marked the western boundary of Cheyenne territory. For this reason alone, Sis-ki-dee reminded himself, the tall proud 'shaman' would soon be confronting him once again.

A slow rage simmered inside him as Sis-ki-dee recalled the time, two winters gone now, when he had suffered the only defeat of his life at the hands of that Noble Champion of Red Pride. Sis-ki-dee challenged him, in front of all the miners and all of Sis-ki-dee's braves, to a Blackfoot Death Hug— a knife fight from which no one can run away because the combatants's free arms were lashed together at the wrists.

The Death Hug was supposed to be a fight to the death. But the Cheyenne had humiliated him by defeating him, but refusing to make the kill. In Sis-ki-dee's eyes, this was equivalent to saying that he was beneath killing—no more threat than a weak-brain or a sick old woman. Though Sis-ki-dee's men still obeyed his orders today, the Blackfoot Renegade knew he would never regain their unswerving loyalty until he killed that Cheyenne.

No, Sis-ki-dee reminded himself. Simple killing would be the last resort of desperation. For he had already make his promise to this Cheyenne, this licker of Crooked Feet crotches, a promise he fully intended to keep: With the Cheyenne alive to see it, he would flay off his prisoner's facial skin and don it like a mask. His enemy would die with his vanquisher's eyes mocking him from his own face.

But the Contrary Warrior pushed thoughts of the Cheyenne from his mind. After all, Wolf Who Hunts Smiling's sound plan would indeed accomplish much more than merely kill their mutual enemy. The wily Cheyenne plotter was right, this place represented a fortune. True, red men had no use for unsmelted gold ore. However, they had plenty of use for other riches at this camp: ready cash for the payroll; fine weapons and equipment; generous stores of food and liquor and coffee. Sis-ki-dee was beginning to believe that this plan for a Renegade Nation might indeed be one to examine.

As for these miners, the company itself, and its richest vein, were located on land claimed by Crooked Feet as part of Wyoming Territory, not Indian grantland. But in order to pack the ore out to Laramie, they had built a railroad spur line connecting with the Great Northern-Platte River line. This line crossed Cheyenne land and had been sighted through for the whites by Touch the Sky.

Bile erupted up Sis-ki-dee's throat as—in spite of his resolve—he again recalled that humiliating defeat. Not just the personal defeat during the Death Hug; Sis-ki-dee and his men had also been thwarted in their efforts to destroy the miners. But again he drove it out of his mind with difficulty. He must concentrate on this huge camp below, for only by learning it might he destroy it.

31

It did not take the Blackfoot long to conclude that this was not the same camp he and his band had once before terrorized. Though many tents remained, there were just as many small but serviceable buildings of yellow pine, most still so new he could smell the pitch from here.

Almost every building was loopholed for defensive firing. The fortifications showed true military genius. Sis-ki-dee admired the log fences with sharp projecting spikes, clearly intended to ruin a massed charge by horses or men. Deep fire-breaks surrounded the camp, and most of the timber and brush had been razed to reduce natural tinder. Any spot that might admit a sizable force was obstructed by huge boulders or sharp-pointed breastworks.

If not exactly a fortress, this reinforced position on high ground was nonetheless a formidable bastion. No sane man, red or white, would try to take it—certainly not with a band that numbered only thirty warriors.

No sane man . . . but the Contrary Warrior was crazy-by-thunder and never did what sane Indians advised. Sane Indians licked white man's spittle for a pinch of snuff. Crazy Indians like Sis-ki-dee paid tribute to no man and took what was there for the taking.

This camp could indeed be taken. For one thing, Sis-ki-dee had one trait in common with the Comanche named Big Tree: his scorn for the Warrior Way so holy to tribes like the Cheyenne and the Sioux, with their rigid code of honorable conduct. Sis-ki-dee eschewed battlefield tactics in favor of a war of nerves, a game wherein he drove his enemies mad with fright and confusion and un-relenting terror.

For another thing, an Army munitions train would soon pass by this place, one that Sioux scouts east of the Black Hills had watched being loaded. Wolf Who Hunts Smiling had learned of it through the Moccasin Telegraph. Sis-ki-dee made a point of learning white men's explosives, and thus he recognized what that train was carrying. And because the Contrary Warrior wisely hoarded tools such as crowbars, stopping that train would be easy. It would pass west of Register Cliffs in the dead of night, hitting top speed as it descended the long headland above the Platte. Sis-ki-dee knew of a dog-leg turn where torn-up tracks would never be spotted in time.

Of course it would be dangerous. At least one car contained the blasting gelatin called nitroglyc-erin, which could be very explosive upon concussion. That train had also been loaded with the new Requa rifle battery, a surprisingly portable weapon with 25 barrels arranged horizontally. It was designed to fire seven volleys per minute, 175 shots. Indians back east had seen white men stop huge charges with these guns, as well as inflict many casualties upon men trapped in groups. These weapons could easily be put into place above the camp, barrels trained downward.

The train also carried weapons called Adams hand grenades. The thrower wore a wrist strap at-tached to a priming pin. Throwing the grenade pulled the pin from the shell to ignite a fuse. True, sometimes the pin did not emerge smoothly, and the live grenade could end up at the thrower's feet.

But this thought made Sis-ki-dee grin. For truly, no Indian flirted with Death so fondly as he. And those grenades, hurled from the peaks and trap-rock shelves above the hollow, would soon have the residents of this Crooked Feet enclave balanced on the feather edge of terror.

The Cheyenne, thanks to Big Tree's efforts down in Bighorn Falls, would not be on hand this time to save Caleb Riley and his men. By the time he did show up, blood vengeance in his eyes, Sis-ki-dee would have the leisure to toy with him—assuming that Big Tree did not first enjoy the pleasure of killing him.

Sis-ki-dee had seen enough for now. It was time to return to Wendigo Mountain, site of the new combined camp, and plan that train strike with his men.

The Red Peril was about to turn his sabino roan when he spotted the two women below.

Sis-ki-dee was not one to waste time admiring beauty in a woman. He took those he wanted, ugly or not, for all dogs barked alike at night. But this pair of beauties could make a rock take notice. The stunning Crow maiden he recognized instantly as Caleb Riley's wife. As for the white woman, he had never seen her before in his life.

She wore the hoop skirts currently fashionable, with a low-crowned, wide-brimmed straw hat to save her complexion. The thick, wheat-colored hair was tied in a heavy knot on her nape and tucked into a silver net. Now he realized who she must be: the sun-haired woman whom the tall Cheyenne had once held in his blanket for love talk.

Sis-ki-dee grinned, his smallpox-scarred face hideous in the harsh afternoon light glinting off the big brass rings in his ears. So the rough-and-tumble camp had become so civilized that they were importing delicate beauties such as these? Only now did Sis-ki-dee really notice all the children playing throughout camp. Spotting them only made his grin wider. For he had once shocked a mother to death by braining her puling baby against a tree.

With women and children on hand this time, Sis-ki-dee assured himself, the war of terror was already won.

Chapter Three

"Brothers," Wolf Who Hunts Smiling said to Swift Canoe and Medicine Flute, "we have made the he-bear talk long enough. Now it is time to either send Woman Face across the Great Divide or ruin him forever in the eyes of our people. As for sending him over, I have done my best by bringing the Contrary Warrior and Big Tree together in one camp. Now it is up to you, Medicine Flute, to ensure his ruin."

This announcement was serious enough to cause Medicine Flute to cease playing the monotonous notes on his leg-bone instrument. He pulled it from his lips and looked at his leader with heavy-lidded eyes, paling slightly.

"Ensure his ruin? I? Buck, have you eyes to see? My 'magic' would fit in the parfleche of a gnat! I have been impressing the fools in this camp with sleight-of-hand and false vision trances. But he has medicine, true medicine!"

The three Cheyenne youths had met in Wolf Who Hunts Smiling's tipi. They were still very early in the warm moons, and the air held a knife edge of chill at night. A fire blazed in the pit. Wolf Who Hunts Smiling was obsessed with ensuring privacy while he hatched his nefarious schemes. Therefore, the tipi wall was ingeniously 'wain-scoted' with thick layers of tanned buckskin to a height of about ten hands. This made it difficult for observers to know how many people were inside after sunset and also muffled the sound of speech.

"You white-livered woman!" Wolf Who Hunts Smiling raged at Medicine Flute. "You skinny, bone-blowing coward! Swift Canoe here is as stupid as the south end of a horse. But he is keen for sport when the war cry sounds. Listen to you. Not once have you been asked to raise a weapon, and still you cower at the rear like a Ponca in his garden!"

"Insult me all you wish," Medicine Flute replied stiffly. "I have never bragged about how I like war and hard work. Let other fools lose their hair fighting useless battles over 'honor.' I would rather eat well from someone else's labor and be warm and coddled when the short white days blow snow into the tipis."

"True it is that I may be stupid," Swift Canoe said. "But even a rabbit has brains enough to like the sound of this. Medicine Flute, may I train as your assistant? Perhaps—"

"I have no ears for your foolish words," Wolf

Who Hunts Smiling snapped, cutting Swift Canoe short. "Do not force me onto my hind legs, either of you. I am a Bull Whip soldier and Lone Bear's favorite. Show some respect and obedience, both of you, or you'll soon taste forty knotted-thong whips."

"Every cock crows on its own dunghill," Medicine Flute said defiantly. "Do as you will. Without me, you will have no Renegade Nation. Who controls a tribe's medicine controls the tribe. If you are so fond of Swift Canoe, then set *him* up as your shaman. You heard him just now, how eager he is to be our medicine man."

These words made Wolf Who Hunts Smiling seethe with silent rage. But wisely he kept his feelings out of his face. For all that Medicine Flute infuriated him, the skinny and lazy brave had indeed proved valuable in the effort to turn the tribe against White Man Runs Him.

"I need you for my plan," he agreed, "but only if you will act like a man. Now have ears for my words. You already know that, soon, Big Tree will have Woman Face's paleface parents locked in the hurt dance. Count upon it, he will not forsake them, for white dogs are loyal to their masters.

"Your part in it is simple and calls only for the skills in which you are adept, the deceptive arts. You must claim a new medicine vision. One which augers that White Man Runs Him will soon, once again, desert his tribe to be with hair faces."

"It sounds simple, I admit." Medicine Flute nodded toward his weakly muscled right thigh and the knot of scar tissue there. "But look on this. The time when we were going to attack the white man's church—he worked medicine on our ponies and drove them Wendigo. My flute snapped and skewered my leg, you yourself suffered a broken leg. Only Swift Canoe here was not injured."

"Bent words," Swift Canoe protested. "My horse threw me and my head struck a tree."

"As I said, you were not injured, though it destroyed the tree."

"You two jays quit this woman's chatter," Wolf Who Hunts Smiling snapped at them. But something had occurred to him, and now he turned to Medicine Flute. "I have noticed a thing. I have noticed how you sigh and stare whenever Honey Eater is within your sight."

"As would any brave," Swift Canoe cut in. "She—"

A withering glance from Wolf Who Hunts Smiling silenced his lickspittle. He looked at Medicine Flute again. "Does she stir your blood?"

"Are beavers rare above the timberline? Of course she stirs my blood. Are *you* not in rut for her?"

"A true warrior, Cheyenne, is never mastered by desires. But of course she is a comely woman, and when the time comes I plan to enjoy her. As might you."

Now Medicine Flute looked far more interested. "It is not your way to speak in riddles, Panther Clan. Say it straight."

"Is this straight enough? With Touch the Sky either dead or driven out, this tribe is ours. Thus, so are the women. Big Tree's Comanches take as many wives as they wish, and may kill any of them for cause. In our new Renegade Nation, many of these fine Comanche laws will prevail. But of course, it requires your help."

Medicine Flute thought about all this. Then, a sleepy grin dividing his face, he nodded. "As you say, brother. I will soon announce my new vision."

When he had a serious problem to study, Touch the Sky liked to work his pony in the huge common corral.

He had several good ponies on his string, all wild mustangs captured in the high country: a quick little piebald good for the long run; a sturdy claybank that could climb mountain trails where only mules could go; a beautiful bay he reserved for riding in the Sun Dance parade and other ceremonies. But his favorite was a powerful chestnut mare with "medicine hat" markings: black speckles throughout her coat, considered good luck by all Indians.

He lunged her now, running her in circles with a long halter to burn off energy. But his mind was on the grizzly claws hanging around his neck. Arrow Keeper had appeared to Honey Eater in a dream and told her to make the necklace! And then there was the dream warning spoken to him in the old shaman's gravelly voice: *For the battle now coming, red man's magic will guard one flank, white man's cunning the other.*

What, he pondered yet again, could be the meaning of it?

Abruptly, cold, sharp steel kissed his throat, and Touch the Sky went as still as stone. He glanced down and saw a hand holding a twine-handle knife.

"Good thing, brother," Little Horse said behind him, "that I am not one of your enemies. It is a rare occasion when any brave can sneak up on you. This tells me that you have trouble firmly by the tail."

Touch the Sky turned to face Little Horse and Tangle Hair. Both braves had recently been sent out by Spotted Tail, their new war chief, to scout the outlying regions. This was the time of year when Apaches and Kiowas and Comanches liked to send raiding parties north to steal good horses.

"If trouble was good grass," Touch the Sky admitted, "our ponies could graze all winter."

Little Horse and Tangle Hair exchanged a long glance. Only now did the preoccupied Touch the Sky notice that his friends, too, looked worried.

"I fear," Little Horse said, "that we can only add to your troubles, brother."

"We three know by now," Touch the Sky told him, "that my troubles are yours too. You two and Two Twists have insisted upon that. And I confess I have been expecting bad news, for the signs and portents have been everywhere. So tell me, stout warriors. What new trouble has ridden our way?"

Touch the Sky spoke straight-arrow—he had indeed been waiting for bad news. But even prepared as he was, Little Horse's blunt reply sent cold blood into his face.

"Tangle Hair and I rode north to the Sans Arc range. While skirting Caleb Riley's mining camp, we saw a lone Indian studying the area for a long time. I rode closer to identify his tribe. But truly, one sight of *this* one was all I needed. For, brother, our enemy Sis-ki-dee has returned."

Deeply troubled, Touch the Sky turned away and untied the chestnut's halter, turning her out to graze again. Then, for a long time, he stood perfectly still and stared out toward the sawtooth pattern of the Sans Arcs, visible to the west. Among the many people in that mining camp whom he called friend was Kristen Steele, hired by Caleb to teach at the camp school. True, Touch the Sky was now married, and Kristen was growing close to Caleb's brother Tom. But Kristen had been his first love. And how many times had she defied her father's deadly wrath to help Touch the Sky?

Finally the deeply worried brave ended his long silence. "He was watching the mining camp?"

"Brother, he was like a cat on a rat. He studied it long."

Touch the Sky turned around to face his friends. "Sis-ki-dee is not one for idle curiosity. If he is watching that camp, then count upon it, his thoughts are nothing but bloody."

"We never thought anything else, Bear Caller," Tangle Hair said grimly. He used the name invented by Little Horse after Touch the Sky had summoned a grizzly bear at Medicine Lake, panicking a band of Pawnee braves who were about to kill him.

"I will say it before you do," Little Horse added. "If Sis-ki-dee is camped in the Sans Arcs, then he will be at the peak of Wendigo Mountain. We defeated him there once before and got our Arrows back. Now he is daring us to rout him again."

"You know him well, brother." Touch the Sky gazed thoughtfully down the long, grassy slope toward their camp in the river valley. The tipis were erected by clan circles, branch frameworks tightly covered with tanned elk and buffalo skins. All entrances faced east toward the rising sun. He glanced toward the Panther Clan circle, his eyes searching out Wolf Who Hunts Smiling's lodge.

"Caleb will have to be warned," he said. "And brothers, Arrow Keeper once told me trouble comes in clusters. Do you recall now some of the sly remarks our wily wolf and the skinny bone blower have been planting throughout camp lately? Sis-ki-dee alone is trouble enough for ten sky-gods. But we had better tend to our battle rigs and give our gifts to the Arrows, for this murdering devil is only part of the poisonous brew."

He met each of his companions in the eye and held them, for his next words were important and they must feel the weight of them if they were to survive.

"Brothers, this place hears me and so do you. We have been up against it before, and though we fear death, none of us is afraid to die. Yet, we must *not* die, for if we do our loved ones are lost. Cheyennes, this time will not be like all the other fights. For *this* time, I fear, our wily wolf has outdone himself in treachery. Bucks, know this. Now comes the battle of all battles."

Old Knobby idly dug at a tick in his grizzled beard while he studied the mirror flashes.

"Hard to kallate," he muttered to the half-wild mustangs grazing at a wary distance from him. "Could just be the moccasin telegraph. But this child figgers there's damn few tribes roll out this soon after sunrise. 'Cept when they're on the annual hunt or the warpath."

The former mountain man stood in a lush gamma-grass meadow that marked the northern boundary of John and Sarah Hanchon's mustang ranch. Squinting to get the best use of his tuckered old eyeballs, he stared toward a distant bluff overlooking the summer pastures. Again he saw several quick flashes of light.

"I swan, it's mighty damn early for redskins to be at it," he assured the horses again. "The Injin is a lazy sumbitch and a late sleeper. This hoss never seed 'em so close to these diggin's. They're up to some sheconnery or I'll be et fir a tater. But which bunch is it?"

Old Knobby had finally fallen victim to the 'rheumatic,' as he called it. But he still wore fringed buckskin shirt and trousers with a slouch beaver hat that had seen far better days. Until recently the crusty old trapper had lived over the boarding stable in nearby Bighorn Falls, serving as the town's hostler for years.

But his penchant for strong forty-rod whiskey, and advancing age, had finally cost him his job. Because of Old Knobby's steadfast loyalty to their adopted Cheyenne son, Matthew, the Hanchons had refused to let him end his days like some old plug in a rendering plant. They had given him permanent title to a snug little line shack up in the high pastures.

Now his only job was to apply his considerable horse sense with the more rebellious mustangs, to occasionally advise one of the younger wranglers on some fine point of breaking green horses to leather. Grateful to the Hanchons for their faith in him, Old Knobby now restricted himself to his "thrice-daily tipple."

And the old trapper had no intention of letting anyone—white men or red—deal any more serious misery to the Hanchons. They had already gone through six sorts of hell to save this place from Hiram Steele and Seth Carlson's attempt to destroy them. And their enemies would've succeeded, too, if young Matthew hadn't come down from the Powder River country and showed them a real by-god war whoop.

Knobby lifted his slouch hat off and swiped at the sweat beading on his forehead. A patch of hideless bone glowed at his crown, the legacy of his days as a wild young buck. The Cheyenne warrior who tried to lift his top-knot had learned first-hand about the white man's fondness for little hideout guns.

"Which tribe is it?" he muttered again.

Suddenly, even as he stared, a lone rider appeared on the bluff. His magnificent ginger turned sideways for a moment. Long enough for Old Knobby, who knew Indians as he knew whiskey and women, to recognize the brightly died roadrunner skin tied to the pony's bushy tale.

"Shit-oh-dear," he said out loud, his face draining pale above his grizzled beard.

This wasn't the moccasin telegraph. This was the tribe that had the dubious distinction of killing more white men than any other. They came this far north for only two reasons: to steal horses or to kill white settlers. And if they were here to steal horses, they would have done it in darkness and been gone by now.

"Comanches," Old Knobby said out loud. And though he was poor shakes at being a Christian, the old salt added with urgent reverence, "Lord help us all!"

Chapter Four

Accompanied by Little Horse, Touch the Sky rode out of camp soon after sunrise only one sleep after receiving the ominous scouting report about Sis-ki-dee. He was determined to warn Caleb Riley and the others at the mining camp as soon as possible. Indeed, knowing how Sis-ki-dee operated, he feared that warning might already be too late.

"Brother," Little Horse said, "did you see how some of the Bull Whips watched us as we rode out? Already tongues are wagging because we did not seek the sanction of council."

"No time," Touch the Sky replied tersely. "While we defend ourselves from the charges of Wolf Who Hunts Smiling and his minions, Sis-ki-dee might make his move. And truly, does it matter what I say in council? For those who believe me are already on my side; those who do not believe

47

me hate me forever and are not likely to change horses now in midstream. White men call it preaching to the converted and call it a waste of time. And this time white men are right."

Little Horse examined these words for some time and then nodded. "Straight words, buck. Why push if a thing will not move? You have taken the peace road with Wolf Who Hunts Smiling and the rest. But to such men as they, covered with hard bark while lacking the true warrior's compassion, gestures of conciliation are seen as womanly weakness."

"Straight-arrow, Little Horse, and well said. There was a time, long before he turned traitor to his own tribe, when Wolf Who Hunts Smiling had better mettle in him. He could have shot me point-blank when he had me under the gun near Medicine Lake. But I had just saved him and Swift Canoe from Pawnees, and he refused to murder me in cold blood."

"That better man is as dead as a Paiute grave," Little Horse said. "You have seen with your own eyes what I have seen. You have seen Wolf Who Hunts Smiling parley with Sis-ki-dee and Big Tree. You know, as I and Two Twists and Tangle Hair alone know with you, that Wolf Who Hunts Smiling once stole our Medicine Arrows and gave them to Sis-ki-dee. And though we have no proof to place in a parfleche, you know as do I that it was our wily wolf who murdered a certain person."

Little Horse refused to name the dead Black Elk, for Cheyennes, like many Indian tribes, believed that the dead might hear their names and answer back.

"Only one mistake," Touch the Sky said, "in all you just spoke. One other person in camp also knows of this treachery, and she is there now among those who value her life less than a gnat's."

"You mean Honey Eater, brother. I did not forget her. Did you notice that neither Tangle Hair nor Two Twists protested when you ordered them to stay behind? I have already talked to them about your wife's safety—as I have talked to Spotted Tail, River of Winds, and certain others about her safety when none of us can be around her. Count upon it, Cheyenne. As long as you have a friend in Gray Thunder's camp, she has a protector night and day."

For a moment, watching his quiet little friend scan the plains around them with an impassive face as he said all this, Touch the Sky's throat pinched shut with deep affection. Because these words were terribly important, Little Horse expected no thanks or appreciation. Indeed, he wanted the subject dropped. Talking about bad luck could make it happen.

"I have noticed," Touch the Sky remarked, keeping his tone just as casual, "that marriage often changes a brave's friendships, that former acquaintances are replaced with newer. For my own part, I have noticed no such thing. I have noticed only that my friends now take care of two where once they watched over one."

"It is natural when two become one. Not one of your friends does not owe his life to you."

But by silent accord, both braves fell quiet as

the plains gave way to the rolling foothills of the Sans Arc range. Now it was time to apply one of the earliest lessons of their warrior training: avoid talking and listen instead to the language of the senses.

It still cankered at Touch the Sky, this sense that the full extent of his new troubles had yet to be revealed. This was particularly daunting when he already knew he would soon face the Blackfoot Contrary Warrior Sis-ki-dee—trouble enough by himself for ten good braves. So far neither the Cheyenne nor the Blackfoot had clearly gained the upper hand in their personal battle. But it troubled Touch the Sky to realize that Sis-ki-dee carried a deep personal grudge, for such men were double danger.

As Sis-ki-dee soon reminded him.

The two Cheyennes had negotiated the foothills without incident, entering the pristine wilderness of the mountains. This was the same awesome and beautiful country through which Touch the Sky had driven the numbered markers of the spur line. They ascended through fields of blue columbine, so thick and high they could reach down and pluck it without dismounting. The route dipped through valleys lush with mountain laurel and golden crocuses. White-water rivers coursed through them, rainbow colors glinting in the sun when fat trout leaped from the water.

Despite this vast beauty, Touch the Sky sensed the nearness of danger the way a burro senses a snake. He and Little Horse had just finished picking their way around a boulder-strewn gorge when Touch the Sky noticed it: a strange, fluting warble that was like no bird sound he had ever heard.

"I hear it, too, brother," the sharp-eared Little Horse said in a low voice. "I think it came from behind us."

"Count upon it, buck. Each time you hear it, the direction will change."

Sure enough, the next time they heard the warbling noise, it came from in front of them.

A stone plopped to the ground between the two riders. Then another. Sweat beaded on Touch the Sky's forehead. The butt of his Sharps brushed his thigh now and then, secure in its scabbard. He knew he had a primer behind the loading gate and a fresh charge, just as he knew that Little Horse's revolving four-barrel shotgun was battle-ready. But wisely, neither brave went for a weapon.

The next stone bounced off the chestnut's flank and made her shy in fright. Touch the Sky quickly calmed her. Meantime he searched desperately from the corners of his eyes but was unable to spot their tormentor.

"Brother," Little Horse said, his voice strained with his nervousness, "we have the best ears in our tribe. How can this Sis-ki-dee get so close to us like this?"

"How? Go ask the Wendigo how his children are so adept. I can only tell you the why. He is humiliating us, the same way he thinks I humiliated him in the eyes of his followers—by not killing him when I might have. This is Sis-ki-dee's way of counting coup. First he reduces a man to gibbering fear, then he makes him die a hard death. But always he reminds him first: Only when *he* names the time will death come. Hold, brother, and do not let him goad you to fire upon him."

But Sis-ki-dee had tired of playing with stones. It was the custom of Cheyenne men to place special notches in the ends of their feathers to mark their clan or military society. As he belonged to neither, Touch the Sky wore an uncut feather. A moment later, however, a shot rang out and startled the braves and their horses.

Touch the Sky felt the round whang past just over his head. Then Little Horse said grimly, "Brother, you just joined the Wolverine Clan, for Sis-ki-dee has notched your feather with their cut!"

As if the hidden marksman had heard Little Horse, a harsh bray of insane laughter echoed down out of the surrounding rimrock.

"Look at them, Scalp Cane!" Sis-ki-dee said to his favorite among his warriors. "True Cheyennes! I could piss on them and they would pretend it was rain—until I showed myself, and then there would be no pretending about the bullets they would plant in my lights!"

Sis-ki-dee laughed his crazy-by-thunder laugh, brass earrings glinting in the sunlight. He jacked a spent cartridge out of the North & Savage and absently handed the weapon to his lackey. Scalp Cane automatically removed a cleaning rod and a wiping patch from his legging sash and ran the patch through the barrel. He handed the weapon back to his battle chief, who returned it to its buckskin sheath.

The sun, as always, was to his back, putting his

enemies at a disadvantage. Sis-ki-dee could see both of them below him, picking their way through a patch of loose talus.

"Red Peril?"

Sis-ki-dee glanced at his lieutenant. The brave had used a name given to his leader by the white men's newspapers—meant as an insult and therefore, to the Contrary Warrior, worn as a badge of honor. He had earned that name after braining the white infant whose mother had died of shock.

"Well? Would you speak up like a man, or must I coax the words out of you?"

Scalp Cane was a stone-hearted killer who always followed the strongest leader. He would brook this kind of mocking from no man, red or white, except Sis-ki-dee. True, he had watched the Cheyenne Bear Caller finally beat Sis-ki-dee in a vicious knife fight. But how many times had he also watched Sis-ki-dee knock Death from His pony? Just as he believed this tall Cheyenne did indeed ride under the blessing of the High Holy Ones, so Scalp Cane believed that Sis-ki-dee was the chosen warrior of the Wendigo. No man could kill him, that Cheyenne shaman included.

"Only this, Contrary Warrior. Why not kill them now and be done with it? This one slew many of our comrades. You have played with him before like this, only to regret it later. He is not a better man than you, Red Peril. But he is a dangerous man. And that brave with him—I have seen him fight, and I know he has no plans to die in his tipi. I say, kill both of them now."

This was well said, and Sis-ki-dee took no offense. Two of his best warriors, Plenty Coups and Takes His Share, were among the victims of that Cheyenne he-bear.

"You speak straight words, Scalp Cane. Each of us has his weakness, and I freely confess mine. When I hate a man past all hating, I do not have it in me to do him any favors. And a quick death, for a man you hate above all others, is surely a favor. Still . . . perhaps after all you are right this time. It is not only my pride, but the blood of our comrades that must be avenged. Run back to the horses and bring me one of the thunder-stones. But handle it carefully."

Scalp Cane grinned as he rose and started down the slope. "Now you will show me how they work!"

Sis-ki-dee felt a burst of anticipation. The raid on the U.S. Army munitions train had gone off as planned. His band had used crowbars to tear up a section of track just past a blind dog-leg bend west of Register Cliffs. The night train hit it at half-throttle, and the locomotive, tender, and one freight car had derailed. They had murdered the engineer, fireman, telegrapher, and six guards, making off with several Requa artillery batteries, cases of Adam's hand grenades, and nitroglycerin in gelatin packs. Everything except a few of the grenades—which Sis-ki-dee described to his men as thunder-stones—was now safely hidden back on Wendigo Mountain.

Everything, Sis-ki-dee thought now as Scalp Cane scrambled back up to their position, except one nitro pack. He had taken care to plant that himself the night before, infiltrating the mining camp. It would be discovered any time now, much to the horror of the hair-faces in that mining camp.

"Here." Gingerly, Scalp Cane handed over the grenade. It was heavy, steel-encased, and shaped to fit a throwing grip. "How do I make it spit fire?"

"Easily. See this strap, how it stretches? It goes around the wrist, this way. It is like a tether. When the stone reaches the end of it, it will pull out the pin. But when you throw it, you must be careful to watch and make sure the thunder-stone goes out far enough. Sometimes the pin comes out wrong, slowing it so it lands at your feet. I saw this happen when soldiers used these against us in the Bear Paws.

"Now watch. . . . "

Sis-ki-dee made sure the wrist strap was secure. Then he glanced downridge again to see where his enemies were. He scrambled a bit further to his right, Scalp Cane following him.

"We are about to ruin the wily wolf's plan, Scalp Cane. But I think our new ally will forgive us for our insubordination."

Sis-ki-dee drew his right arm back, raising his left and pointing it out before him to help him aim. Then, copper brassards clinking slightly with the toss, he launched the thunder-stone down toward Touch the Sky and Little Horse.

Touch the Sky heard the tiny sound of metal clinking and glanced straight up into the dazzling sunlight. It was impossible to see much more than a vague human shape suddenly duck out of sight. But that split-second warning was enough to prime Touch the Sky to danger when something heavy bounced off the rawhide shield strapped to his rope rigging.

The object bounced high enough for the brave to snake one hand out suddenly to catch it. He had never before seen the new grenades close-up. But thanks to his schooling among the whites, he was able to read just enough letters of the word Explosive. Instead of gripping the object, he struck it as hard as he could with his palm, swatting it over into a pile of scree.

Little Horse was completely baffled when his friend suddenly pounced on him, pulling him off his horse and onto the ground hard.

A heartbeat later, an earsplitting detonation shook the ground beneath them as rock dust blasted them and sent their ponies scrambling in wild-eyed fright.

Chapter Five

Both Cheyenne braves were too stunned, at first, to do more than make sure they still belonged to the land of the living. Then, cutting behind a line of boulders to eliminate easy shots from above, they hurried forward and rounded up their frightened mounts.

"Sis-ki-dee will not leave the caprock," Touch the Sky remarked, his mouth set in its grim, determined slit as he nodded behind them. "We are drawing too near to the mining camp, we should be safe now."

"Brother," said a badly shaken Little Horse, "I know about the bluecoats' big-thundering wagon guns. But what manner of weapon was *that*?"

"Buck, I know not. But it has fallen into the hands of the worst possible red devil of them all."

"Only think," Little Horse said. "Just after we

rode out, we saw the smoke from the Sioux camp near Beaver Creek. The message about the iron horse that jumped from its path?"

Despair washed over Touch the Sky as he realized Little Horse must be right. According to reports from the moccasin telegraph, that was a weapons train; obviously whatever was on it was now in their enemy's hands—to be turned against them and the miners.

"It is as you said," Little Horse noted grimly, watching all around them with a nervous eye. "This time, you said, would come the battle of all battles. Now we know why it will be hard."

"Sadly, stout Indian, I fear we still have not tasted all the bloody brew they have concocted for us. Wolf Who Hunts Smiling has more surprises in his parfleche. Little Horse, it was your example that turned Two Twists so scornful of death. You will need your famous boasts now more than ever."

This coaxed a bit of color back into the warrior's face. He grinned. "I confess the noise frightened me more than the prospect of dying. Brother, I hold you second to no warrior. But you will never believe, as I must, that a bad death is repeated eternally. It is not merely dying, but the fear of a bad death, that puts ice on my limbs. These whiteskin weapons will not even let a man die quietly."

Thus their courage was somewhat restored by the time they were within hailing distance of the mining camp. The headframe of the mine itself was visible further up the side of the mountain. A narrow-gauge railway for pushing small ore cars connected with the spur line below in camp. Touch the Sky spotted the diamond smokestack of the locomotive used to haul the ore into Register Cliffs. Ernie Hupenbecker, the engineer, shouted good-natured taunts at the halfbreed boy who served as his fireman, frantically shovelling coal into the boiler to build up steam pressure.

The halfbreed spotted the two Cheyennes approaching. He leaped down off the locomotive and scuttled to the open doorway of a hewn-plank building marked *office* on a shingle over the door. A moment later, a grinning Caleb Riley came out into the street to meet them.

"It's my pathfinder!" he greeted Touch the Sky in English. "Hail fellow well met! Cookie just whipped up some tolerable beef dodgers and buckwheat cakes. Swing down off your ponies and come eat white man's chuck again."

Tom Riley's younger brother Caleb was a big-framed man sporting a full blond beard. He wore the new riveted Levi's and a store shirt with buttons as well as a miner's helmet with a squat candle mounted in front. While he was still greeting the new arrivals, they were joined by his mine captain, Liam McKinney, a burly redhead in twill coveralls.

Over hot food and coffee sweetened with condensed milk, Touch the Sky broke the grim news to Caleb and Liam, occasionally pausing to translate something for Little Horse, who spoke no English: Their archenemy, Sis-ki-dee, had returned, and evidently he and his renegades were packing U.S. Army explosives this time.

"From what you said, I'd guess that was an

Adam's hand grenade you had your brush with," Caleb said. "We've got one of them Beardslee portable telegraph units now. I'll wire Register Cliffs and find out exactly what was taken from that train. Then we'll at least know what we're up against."

"I'll tell you right now what we're up against, boyo," Liam said. "One mean damn Injin, that's what. He had us trapped between shit and sweat once before even without no damned explosives. What'll he be like this time? Oh, we got a tit in the wringer, lads! And just when we opened a new stope and've got production up to snuff."

"Calm down, you big Irish sot. I wasn't born in the woods to be scared by an owl."

But Caleb's heart didn't seem to be in his brave words. Touch the Sky knew what the young miner was thinking: about all the good men Sis-ki-dee and his murdering renegades had sent across the Great Divide the last time they terrorized this camp. And now it wasn't just men in danger, but their families as well.

Touch the Sky was holding this last thought as he glanced out under the open fly of the tent. The picture of beauty that met his eye nearly struck the breath from him.

They stood side by side, Kristen Steele and Caleb's Crow Indian wife, Woman Dress. Kristen wore the wide crinoline now in fashion with white women, her wheat-colored hair worn long over one shoulder under a straw Gypsy hat. As for Woman Dress, she exhibited all the traits that made Crow women among the most beautiful on the Plains: clear skin, almond-shaped eyes, brilliant black hair worn down below her buttocks.

For a moment, his eyes following Touch the Sky's, Caleb lost his deep frown. "Looks like a painting, doesn't it? The two of them have become best friends. I confess I wasn't too sweet on the idea when my brother Tom asked me to hire on Kristen as our teacher. But she's good for the kids *and* for Woman Dress."

Little Horse followed none of the English. But Touch the Sky knew it was bothering him, this sight of Kristen. Little Horse greatly admired the white woman's pluck and courage in standing up to Hiram Steele. But he also knew that, at one time, Touch the Sky had held her in his blanket for love talk. Little Horse's loyalty to Honey Eater now made him fidget.

However, more pressing matters claimed their attention as the halfbreed runner soon returned with a telegram for Caleb, the response from Register Cliffs.

Caleb read it silently, then passed it over to Touch the Sky. The Cheyenne read the brief message, then met his white friend's eyes. "I know about nitro, and I've just been introduced to the hand grenades. What's a Requa battery?"

"Tom keeps up on all these new-fangled weapons. He told me it's called a covered-bridge gun back east because it can stop an enemy charge across a bridge. Think of it as the firepower of an entire cavalry platoon, concentrated into one weapon. It's light, portable, easy to hide."

Little Horse stoically maintained an impassive face as Touch the Sky translated all this. "Is there sugar for the coffee?" he said calmly, and now

Judd Cole

Touch the Sky understood, grinning. His friend was slightly embarrassed for losing his bravado earlier, when the grenade caught them.

"A Requa gun will wake snakes, all right," Liam agreed. "But that nitro is the boy we want to give the slip to. Hell, we just need to *look* at it wrong and we'll be knocked into a cocked hat!"

All four men were heading out of the tent by now.

"Production will continue," Caleb said determinedly. "We aren't as tender as we were the first time that savage bastard braced us. We'll set up picket outposts around the camp at night. During the day, we'll keep patrols going all around this area.

"We'll take precautions with the women and kids, of course. Unfortunately, we can't count on much help from the Army. Fort Bates is a full day's ride to the southeast. Tom is gone right now, assigned to extended scouting duty down in the canyonland. But he tells me this new commanding officer at the fort is crooked as cat shit—in tight with the Indian Ring back in Washington. He's got no interest in fighting, only in collecting on lucrative contracts to supply the tribes."

While Caleb was speaking, Kristen spotted Touch the Sky and Little Horse. A wide smile divided her face and, taking Woman Dress by the hand, she hurried toward them.

But Touch the Sky didn't smile back. For just then his shaman sense prodded at him, as real as a hand on the back of his neck.

"Brother?" Little Horse said, seeing the look in his friend's eye and knowing what it meant. He added quietly, "What is it, Bear Caller?"

Touch the Sky shook his head, glancing all around. Now he spotted Ernie again, just then venting the boilers of the locomotive. The old Dutchman spotted the two Cheyennes and hit the chain of his whistle, greeting them with a blast of steam. In spite of his habit of keeping feelings out of his face, Little Horse grinned like a young boy as he recalled his first ride in the powerful iron horse. How he had fed coal to its fiery maw, and how it had hungered for more! He started toward it.

"Ernie runs into Register Cliffs with a full load about every other day now," Caleb bragged, momentarily forgetting his new troubles. "Top-grade ore. This operation is some pumpkins!"

But again the warning was back, making Touch the Sky glance about desperately. Kristen and Woman Dress had closed the gap when Touch the Sky noticed it: a canvas-covered square about the size of a preacher's Bible. It was tucked up under the drive wheel of the locomotive that was about to back onto its siding to turn around.

"Little Horse!" he commanded. "Stop where you are!"

Ernie hit the whistle again, and suddenly Touch the Sky understood what that object under the wheel must be.

"Ernie! Stop!"

But the old Dutchman only cupped one hand over his ear, unable to hear the Indian's shouts over the hiss of a full head of steam. He hit the reverse lever, engaging the drive wheel.

The iron horse shuddered, then groaned into motion.

"Brother?" said a confused Little Horse. "What—?"

The next moment, Ernie Hupenbecker's entrails sprayed out of the cab, and the huge locomotive was literally lifted into the air by a crack-booming explosion that made Touch the Sky believe the end of Creation was at hand.

Chapter Six

The Comanche war leader named Big Tree had killed his first Cheyenne warrior back when the rugged mountain men known as the Taos Trappers still hired scouts to lead them into the north country. Since then only one Cheyenne had ever bested him in battle, though even that one had been unable to kill him.

Clearly, this thing could not stand. Of all the tribes to the north that had driven his people to the desolate southwest deserts, he hated the Cheyennes the most. They had killed his father in the famous battle at Wolf Creek, and they had slain Big Tree's leader, Hairy Wolf, right before his startled eyes.

But now Big Tree swore to the sun and the earth he lived on that the arrogant Cheyenne warrior named Touch the Sky would soon touch the ground—never to rise from it again.

The Comanche sat his ginger mustang just beneath the crest of a razorback ridge overlooking the Hanchon spread. Below him, the lush bottomland rose gradually into gentle hills dotted with stands of juniper and scrub pine. He could clearly see the log-and-stone main house, the bunkhouse and outbuildings of raw pine. Several wranglers worked green mustangs in a breaking pen. Big Tree's stern face creased in a smile when he noticed all the tall hayricks dotting the ranch.

Big Tree was of good size for a Comanche, though he had the characteristic bowed legs that were only at home on horseback. He also had the oval face and center-parted hair typical of his tribe. Big Tree was a member of the Quohada, the elite Antelope Eaters Band, which boasted only one motto: *Revenge is a dish best served cold*. Patiently, while he waited for his next meeting with the arrogant shaman, he had honed the battle skills that made him the most feared Comanche in the Southwest.

His shield was embedded with mirror glass so that, attacking into the sun, he could blind his opponent. In the time it took a blue soldier to load and fire a carbine twice, Big Tree could ride his ginger 300 yards while stringing and firing 20 arrows with deadly accuracy. The Comanches were the "natural jockeys" of the Plains, bouncing along with perilous ease during battle, seldom needing to guide their ponies—ponies trained as sharp as circus mounts, and each brave with five or more on his string.

And those hair-mouthed squaw men below—

hay-growers and dust-scatterers, he thought with contempt—were about to taste his battle prowess. Just a touch. The point was to gradually build terror so that eventually word would be sent north to the tall shaman, warning him that his whiteskin parents were up against a villain worthy even of Sis-ki-dee's reputation.

Big Tree whirled his pony and trotted back downridge to the spot where his band of fifteen battle-hardened warriors waited. He wore captured bluecoat trousers and boots. He was bare from the waist up except for a bone breastplate. Like the rest of his men, his face was painted in battle colors: vertical green and yellow stripes.

"War Pipe!" he called. "Buffalo Hump! Stone Fist! You three, ready some fire arrows, then check your battle rigs. When the sun has traveled the width of three lodge poles, we will strike!"

"It fair gives *this* hoss the fidgets," Old Knobby insisted. "They wasn't just curious. That-air buck was a Comanche, and you can't trust a Comanche any sooner than you can catch a weasel asleep. I swan, they're up to some shecoonery."

Old Knobby and John Hanchon sat across from each other at a deal table. While they talked, Sarah moved back and forth between a big iron cookstove and the table, heaping their plates with bread, potatoes, and side meat. The kitchen was spacious and airy and smelled of strong ash soap and sourdough mash.

"Pretty far north for Comanches," John said thoughtfully, sipping from a mug of strong, hot tea. From outside came the steady racket of hammering. John pulled a watch from his vest and thumbed back the cover. He whistled. "Just a hair past seven o'clock, and already Corey's working on them breaking chutes! That boy is pure ambition. Unlike that damned, lazy, stump-screaming pa of his."

"John," Sarah rebuked him gently. "Corey's pa is a preacher. Maybe he is a bit intolerant of sinning—being around those god-awful miners did that to him. But don't forget, when Hiram Steele and his thugs were persecuting Matthew for his Indian blood, Corey's father condemned them."

"Now lookit here, you two," Knobby said impatiently. "Never mind Corey's pa. I might be old, but I ain't soft-brained yet! John Hanchon, I fit my first Innun while you was still on ma's milk. You best mark my words about these here Comanch."

John was tempted to grin, but the serious frown on Knobby's face dissuaded him. John was a thickset, middle-aged man wearing sturdy linsey trousers with gallowses instead of a belt. Though a good belly was started, there was also plenty of hard muscle in his chest and arms.

"Now, no need to get all your pennies in a bunch, Knobby. How many times have we ever had any Indian trouble around here? Our trouble has been with white trash like Hiram Steele."

"Trash is trash, son, and it comes in all colors. I understand why you and the missus is slow to get on the peck agin Injuns. Why, I never knowed a finer lad than Matthew. When Steele run him out of town, you two and Corey was mighty low. But one good apple don't make the orchard. I'll say it once more, and you best write it on your pillow case: These Comanches mean bad trouble."

"Hell," John said, "maybe all they want is 'Indian tax.' A cow or two or a few mustangs. Lots of times they'll take that and leave in peace. If that's all this bunch wants, they're welcome to it."

"We don't question your experience, Knobby," Sarah said gently, moving up beside the old man's three-legged stool and placing one hand on his shoulder. She wore her copper hair pulled into a tight bun on the nape of her neck. "Nor your loyalty and concern for us. Matthew told us how you helped him that time when Wes Munro tried to steal the Cheyenne grantland. You could have been killed."

"You're solid bedrock, Knobby," John threw in. "It's just that me and Sarah would rather give these Indians a chance to approach us first before we go starting trouble."

"Mighty Christian of you," Knobby muttered. "Mighty foolish, too. I got no axe to grind agin the red man—this child has learnt plenty from studyin' their ways, and they got their side of the story, too. But I got me a god-fear this time. That Comanch I seed didn't look too hungry, and he was ridin' a fine pony. He ain't lookin' for no Indian tax."

Corey Robinson finished driving a nail and paused for a moment to wipe the sweat off his forehead.

He liked working out here at the Hanchon spread. Ever since Corey had finished his apprenticeship with a carpenter in Bighorn Falls, John Hanchon had tossed plenty of work his way—

whether he could afford to or not. But these days he could definitely afford it. Nearby Fort Bates was a remount post, and there was a constant demand for good horses. Such a demand, in fact, with Hiram Steele run out for good, that John was having several more breaking chutes constructed to meet all the orders.

"Damn shoddy nails," Corey muttered when yet another three-inch nail snapped the first time he tapped it with his hammer. That cinched it: No more supplies from the fort. The new commander at Fort Bates, Corey thought, was nothing but a bent shooter. He was in thick with the fort sutler, and they were salting away a fortune by ordering shoddy goods in bulk while pocketing top government prices for first-rate goods.

Things just went to hell around here after Matthew left, Corey thought as he picked up his adze and began planing the rough edges off another pine board. Not that Matthew had much choice in the matter.

"Why, Christ on a crutch, sprout! You still piddlin' with that first chute?" Old Knobby called out behind him. The old trapper moved at a good clip, though with a marked limp—the legacy of his imprisonment aboard Wes Munro's flatboat. "And you made brags on how you was a carpenter? Why, pee doodles! Let this old hoss show you how to make your beaver."

"Aww, hell with you, you old fartsack," Corey shot back. The pale, freckle-faced redhead flashed his gap-toothed smile. "You old timers all think you're big bugs."

"Tadpole, you be in your prime. *This* child's already had his threescore and ten years, all the Good Book says he gets. But mark me, pup: This buck still pinches titties. Where *you* gettin' your best?"

Knobby roared with laughter, so hard he had to hawk up phlegm, as Corey blushed. "Why, lookit here, she's flushin' like a honeymoon squaw!"

"You old coot," Corey muttered, though a moment later he, too, broke out laughing.

"Jesus, boy," Knobby added when he caught his breath. "I'uz only talkin' about milkin' the damn cows!" They burst out laughing again.

"You greenhorn," Knobby teased him as he handed Corey another board, "if—"

The next word snagged in his throat as, with a solid thwack that jarred the old man's bones, an arrow embedded in the board he was holding— embedded, pierced, struck a fence post, and still punched several inches further.

"God-in-whirlwinds!" Corey exclaimed.

"Ain't God," Knobby shot back. "It's the Devil on a horse, and the Old Gent is loaded for bear! Innuns, boy! Cover down!"

Knobby hadn't even finished speaking when the sudden pounding of hooves approached from the sun. Neither man could make out much by staring that way, only the dark shapes hurtling down on them like a juggernaut of destruction.

One of the Indians, the big one leading them, sent mirror flashes into their eyes, further blinding them. Knobby, unarmed like Corey, leaped behind a serried stack of fence poles. Corey ducked behind the buckboard he used to haul his supplies.

"Innuns!" Knobby shouted with remarkable lung power back toward the hands in the working pens. "Warn the house!"

A wrangler tore off toward the main house. Corey watched, cold sickness filling his stomach, as a Comanche arrow punched clean through the wrangler's neck and dropped him, skidding, onto his face. He writhed like a fish on shore, choking to death on his own blood.

"There's your Indian tax," Knobby muttered with disgust.

But trouble quickly heaped on trouble, all of it happening faster than a hungry man could gulp a biscuit. Now the arrows flying past them were trailing flame and smoke. Again and again, so many the air seemed to hum with them. They embedded in the bunkhouse, the stables, the coops; several even reached the main house. A horse shrieked in pain and buckled to its knees as an arrow punched clean through it.

"Katy Christ!" Knobby said. "Osage wood bows and filed points." He knew a Comanche could put an arrow clean through the wide part of a buff and drop it out the other side.

Despite the hail of deadly arrows, several wranglers bravely darted here and there, tugging the fire arrows out of buildings and beating at the flames with their shirts and jackets. But in less than a minute, a half-dozen huge hayricks were licking at the sky with fiery tongues. Horses panicked, leaping the corral rails and heading back toward the wild country.

Wind whipped up, sending flaming hay everywhere, even the roof of the main house. John Hanchon emerged from the kitchen, a long-barreled Henry in the crook of his arm. But before he could draw a bead, the raiders were fading to the east, already halfway up the sloping wall of the river valley.

"Jesus God!" Corey said, already heading toward the now ominously still wrangler on the ground. "They killed Will Denning!"

"He's dead as last Christmas," Knobby confirmed grimly. "But sprout, this ain't no time to lick our wounds. Look yonder."

Knobby pointed toward the house just as Sarah Hanchon screamed for help. Then Corey felt his face drain cold when he saw six-foot flames dancing on top the house.

Chapter Seven

"Cheyenne people, have ears! A vision has been placed over my eyes by Maiyun, the Good Supernatural!"

Medicine Flute's words rang out with the riveting authority of bluecoat carbines. Sharp Nosed Woman bent closer to Honey Eater and muttered, "Niece, tell me a thing? How is it that skinny weakling can bellow like a bull?"

She made sure to whisper. For even here, in her own clan circle, Medicine Flute and Wolf Who Hunts Smiling had planted their spies. But Honey Eater had no share in her Aunt's scorn. Her immediate response was fear, not disdain. Anytime Medicine Flute claimed the people's attention like this, it was only a harbinger of some new disaster—usually for Touch the Sky.

She and her aunt were pounding sun-dried buffalo meat with mauls. When sufficiently softened, it would be mixed with fat, marrow, and cherry paste to make pemmican. Little of it would be eaten now during the warm moons, when fresh game was plentiful. Rather, it would be the staple of their diet during the cold moons and the short white days to come.

Honey Eater watched Lone Bear, leader of the Bull Whips, call the camp crier to his lodge. Moments later the crier went to cut his pony out of the common corral and began racing through camp, calling everyone to the central clearing to hear Medicine Flute.

Hearing all this commotion, Chief Gray Thunder stepped past the entrance flap of his tipi. For a moment his eyes met Honey Eater's, and she saw the terrible apprehension in his heart reflected there. But also the terrible frustration. Gray Thunder was a good peace chief who had been outflanked by Wolf Who Hunts Smiling's treachery. Now, Honey Eater realized, Gray Thunder no longer had a united tribe. Thus, he could no longer speak as the common voice.

"This is wrong," she told her aunt, making the older woman wince when she refused to lower her voice. "Lone Bear does wrong to use the crier like this. Medicine Flute has not been named by the Council of Forty to any position, neither shaman nor clan leader. He has not even joined a soldier troop! He does not merit such a privilege."

"Hush, not so loud! His followers disagree, niece. And where once he had only a few, now he has a legion! Look at them now, rushing to hear him as if he were a High Holy One. Never forget that many believe deep in their heart of hearts that this skinny one set a star on fire and sent it blazing across the sky."

"I am certainly going to hear him, too," Honey Eater said, placing her work aside and rising from the ground. "Though I already know it will be an attack on my husband. Talk buzzed through the lodges when he rode to the Sans Arcs. I know not what happened there, Aunt, for Touch the Sky would not tell me. But once again he has ridden out without sanction of council. And this time he took not only Little Horse, but Tangle Hair and Two Twists. Since this tribe's best warriors are now gone, its greatest cowards will play the big Indian."

Sharp Nosed Woman rose, too, though she gripped her niece hard by one elbow.

"Shush! Do you see how the people are looking? Child, being the daughter of a great chief once protected you. But do not forget, the younger braves, those under Wolf Who Hunts Smiling's influence, only dimly remember your father. Honey Eater, you now share a tipi with the most hated brave in this village."

"Yes, but the most respected in the eyes of those who are decent and live to keep the Arrows clean."

"True. Gray Thunder admires him greatly. And though he often confuses me, so do I. But if you have eyes to see, then they have seen Gray Thunder's power steadily usurped by Wolf Who Hunts Smiling."

By now they had joined the edge of the throng crowding the central clearing. Several huge cottonwood fires sent fragrant flames high into the black dome of the night sky. Honey Eater's next breath snagged in her throat when she spotted Medicine Flute.

"That dishonest coward!" she exclaimed, forgetting herself. Sharp Nosed Woman cringed when several persons turned to scowl at them.

But Honey Eater could not believe this travesty! Look at him, standing there boldly in the light of a fire—wearing a war bonnet with coup feathers! And look at those dyed scalps adorning his sash! This white-livered coward had never even killed a buffalo, much less an enemy warrior.

Evidently the leader of the Bow String troopers thought so, too. For now Spotted Tail shouted out, "Look, Bow Strings! It must be time for the Animal Dance. Medicine Flute is wearing a costume!"

"Truly!" said another Bow String. "Now I know why I saw him clipping hair from his pony's tail. He has made them into scalps!"

This drew laughter and several more comments from Bow String soldiers. And now Honey Eater noticed something else—where was Wolf Who Hunts Smiling? Surely he would not miss this opportunity to speak against his worst enemy in the world? Only one reason could explain it: Even now he was involved in another plot against Touch the Sky.

"Mock!" Medicine Flute called out. "As Wolf Who Hunts Smiling has said to you, Spotted Tail—your humor is as faint as your manhood."

"Do *you* also question my manhood, bone blower?"

"Silence! We are not a tribe without a chief!" Gray Thunder shouted with booming authority. "I have no ears for this fighting and bickering and clashes of bulls here in the midst of our camp! Medicine Flute, you have gathered us. Now be a man! Speak what you will, that we may go back to our lives."

"Only this, Gray Thunder! Everyone hearing me now knows that White Man Runs Him has—"

"His name," Honey Eater spoke out boldly, "is Touch the Sky, and a 'man' of your kind should say it with fear and respect—if you must say it at all."

This was too bold for many, a woman speaking out like this to a man. And to such a brave as this one, whose medicine could move the stars! Medicine Flute met her eyes.

"No bull worth the name," he told her calmly, "lets the cow bellow to him. Your 'man' has not the strength to teach you humility before your betters. But as for your remark about pronouncing your noble husband's name—soon, perhaps, no one will be pronouncing it."

No one, least of all Honey Eater, could misunderstand the blunt meaning of this. For a long moment cold dread replaced her blood. Before she could recover to speak again, Medicine Flute shot her another droopy-lidded, sinister smile, then addressed himself to the assemblage again.

"Everyone here knows that *Honey Eater's husband* has ridden off to the Sans Arcs. He obtained no vote of the stones for this act, assuring us it was a crucial matter touching on the welfare of our tribe. He insists we will lose our valuable trade goods if he does not assist the gold miners.

"I never believed this, of course. But now I have had a medicine vision. I saw our tribe's future written on the whirlwind, and the face of the whirlwind is the face of Touch the Sky! For I tell you this: Honey Eater's husband is a liar and a traitor. He only rode to the Sans Arcs as a feint. Soon, count upon it, he will slip away quietly to the hair-face village at Bighorn Falls. He is secretly going to join white men, once again, in treachery aimed at stealing our homeland!"

"Production has officially stopped," Caleb Riley said glumly. "For one thing, we're without a locomotive *or* an engineer. And even though most of the men are willing to work, I don't want to risk leaving the women and kids unprotected. That red devil has high-power explosives! I don't dare put this mine on production schedule until we get out from under that Blackfoot bastard's thumb. Meantime, I'm meeting payroll with no ore going out."

Touch the Sky, Little Horse, Tangle Hair, and Two Twists shared Caleb's rude office with the worried young miner. Caleb now wore a long-barreled Smith & Wesson .44, the heavy-frame Cavalry model, holster tied low on his thigh. His men, too, now went everywhere armed.

Touch the Sky translated Caleb's remarks for his companions. Then he turned back to Caleb and spoke in English.

"Fighting Sis-ki-dee is like trying to fight a prairie fire in a windstorm. No matter where you turn, he's there. Plans don't work well against him because he follows no logic. He lives up to his name, the Contrary Warrior. All we can expect is the unexpected."

Touch the Sky knew he faced more than a hard fight from Sis-ki-dee. Bringing his loyal trio to the Sans Arcs without permission of Council meant new troubles were gestating back at the Powder River camp. Nor, as serious as the threat from Sis-ki-dee clearly was, could he shake his conviction that more trouble still loomed.

"We know where his camp is," Touch the Sky said. "But I fear there is nothing he would welcome more than an attempt to rout him and his braves from it. As to that, it would be easier to drive Apaches out of breastworks. Only one trail leads up to their camp, and it is easily defended from above. Ten bluecoat regiments couldn't get up there alive."

"So what the hell do we do?" Caleb said, frustration adding a raw edge to his voice. "Ernie's dead, and four workers were hurt when the locomotive went up. It's a damn miracle that Woman Dress and Kristen were only scared witless. They might not be so lucky next time."

Touch the Sky could gainsay none of this. Nor could he avoid Caleb's point, a point the young Cheyenne didn't want to concede, but had to.

"You're saying we'll *have* to approach that campsite whether we want to or not."

Caleb nodded. "Otherwise, what's the alternative? We just wait for that yellow-bellied sapsucker to pick us off at will. That was a good quantity of munitions he stole from the Army. We've only begun to taste the meal he's got in store for us."

Caleb's urgency was not based solely on the explosion in camp—that same night Sis-ki-dee's band blew up a key trestle two miles from camp. It would have to be rebuilt before any ore could be packed out—and what was the point of rebuilding, so long as Sis-ki-dee remained in the area, armed with nitro and grenades?

By now Touch the Sky's companions, baffled by the language barrier, were again impatient. He described the impasse they had reached. It was Little Horse who made the suggestion.

"Brother, Yellow Beard is right. Now the game is all Sis-ki-dee's. And you, too, speak straight-arrow when you say no force could ascend Wendigo Mountain. But someone must at least go up there and study the camp. Though a force would be doomed, two braves might stand a chance. Especially if those braves were we two."

Though never shy about boasting, this time Little Horse was not bragging, only stating a clear fact. For he and Touch the Sky had already gained the peak of that bad-medicine mountain in spite of Sis-ki-dee's supreme efforts to stop them.

Things were the way they were, and now Touch the Sky nodded agreement. Reluctantly, he told Caleb Little Horse's suggestion.

"I'll go with you," Caleb offered without hesitation. "And don't tell me married men can't go, cuz we're *both* married to beautiful Indians, Touch the Sky."

Touch the Sky shook his head. "You'd be handy to have along, but you've got enough work cut out for you protecting this area. Little Horse and I will go. Tangle Hair and Two Twists will stay here and search the area around camp. If we keep roving sentries out, we might avoid the next explosion."

"Anyhow," Caleb said, "I feel a little better knowing we at least have a plan."

Touch the Sky nodded, saying nothing to this. But secretly, he had no share in Caleb's guarded optimism. Nor could he pretend that his Cheyenne companions didn't feel it the same as he did, for all three of them had scaled that terrifying mountain of death with him.

A man was lucky enough to return once from Wendigo Mountain. Defying that unholy peak twice was a task for suicide warriors.

"Brothers," said a gloating Big Tree, "fate must favor our new Renegade Nation! For truly, this raid down in Bighorn Falls could not have come off better than it did.

"We drew paleface blood and set many fires. Even now my men are still camped near there, waiting to strike again in my absence. The hairface named John Hanchon owns many fine mustangs. But there will be fewer on his string when my braves are done sporting with him."

Wolf Who Hunts Smiling had ears for this. He, Sis-ki-dee, and Big Tree spoke in the familiar mix of Sioux and Cheyenne words that had become the lingua franca of Plains Indians. Seldom were they forced to resort to sign language.

All three watched Sis-ki-dee's men further down the wind-swept face of Wendigo Mountain. They were rolling huge boulders into place to block a vulnerable breach in the natural defenses. Nearer the bare pinnacle, bent-frame wickiups and log dugouts were growing in number as the combined camp began to take formidable shape. Wickiups, because of their low and curving shape, were more practical than tipis in these fierce and constant winds.

"Big Tree," Wolf Who Hunts Smiling said, "I never expected a brave of your prowess to return with any other report."

Sis-ki-dee uttered a harsh bark of scorn. "Listen to these two love birds cooing! They have set hay on fire and ambushed a family lodge. Now they recite their coups like blooded warriors."

Big Tree leveled a cold glance on the Blackfoot. Sis-ki-dee's big North & Savage rifle was still sheathed. But a Blackfoot brave was generally good with a blade, and Sis-ki-dee's bowie had blood gutters carved in it to facilitate rapid bleeding. The crazy glint in Sis-ki-dee's eyes—taunting him, daring him—convinced Big Tree to bide his time with this one. Abruptly, the Comanche smiled.

"Well spoken, Contrary Warrior! But perhaps you will swallow back those words when I kill the Bear Caller!"

"If you do indeed kill him, Big Tree, I will be the first to pay obeisance to you. However, I might sooner see a civet cat top a whip snake! While your braves were squashing pis-mires, mine did the hurt dance on Caleb Riley's miners. The mine stands idle. The women and children huddle in their lodges. The men must feel between their legs to remember their sex, we have them so terrified of the next explosion."

"No more of this clashing of jealous stags," Wolf Who Hunts Smiling said impatiently. "Indeed, you have both done well so far. Only think. Now that we have joined, you two performed like the awl and the thread. *Both* are needed if one would sew."

He glanced downslope again at the braves shoring up the defenses on the only approach to this bastion. The Cheyenne's famous lupine grin abruptly divided his face.

"You have both done well," he repeated. "By now, Medicine Flute has attacked on one front, announcing his 'vision.' Sis-ki-dee's brilliant strategy with the bluecoat explosives has the miners nearly gibbering in fright. Many will desert as even more are killed. Soon this camp will enrich all three of us.

"As for White Man Runs Him, what has he done so far? And count upon it. One more bloody strike on his white parents will lure him south, so that we may pick Caleb Riley's camp clean as we will.

"You two jays squawk over who kills him. I know that one better than you know him, and I tell you only this. Once I, too, swore revenge against him. Once I, too, made loud public boasts about killing him. Now I know better, and I care not *which* of us it is, so it is done. It is not a matter of luxury or even revenge. If we do not send him over we had best sing our own death songs, for the tall one plans to string his next bow with our guts."

Chapter Eight

The four men sat around the breakfast table, their faces serious as death: John Hanchon, Old Knobby, Corey Robinson, and John's foreman, a tough old Appalachian named Evan Blackford.

"They had no call to do what they done," Evan said. "Ain't been no Injin trouble in this holler for quite a spell. I nary fought agin Plains redskins afore, but I helped my pa run Cherokees off our place back home. Naw, hell. I ain't afeared. If they're fixen to come back, I'll toss lead to 'em. But I do wish to Jesus we had a few exter hands what was tolable with a gun. These horse wranglers ain't much for bustin' caps."

"No," John agreed. "A wrangler mostly uses his gun for shooting snakes and signaling. We can't expect this bunch to hold off warriors as skilled as those Comanches."

Judd Cole

Sarah, busy keeping the men's plates piled high with griddlecakes, said, "Why should they have to? That's what the fort is here for."

"You'd think so, wouldn't you?" John said bitterly. "Especially since right now I'm supplying most of their good horseflesh. But I could tell, by the way Colonel Lyman brushed me off when I went to see him, that he doesn't care two jackstraws what happens here."

"Why should he?" Corey said. "That crooked sonofabitch—pardon my range manners, Missus Hanchon—has got a brother-in-law who just came out from the States. He's set himself up in the mustang business over in Red Shale."

John nodded glumly. "I heard. With Tom Riley way the hell down practically in Old Mexico, we don't have friend one at Fort Bates."

"Will's dead and buried," Blackford said. "It leaves a body puny feelin', thinking on how they cut him down. And Jeb Flemming laid up from an arrow through his leg."

"Hell 'n' furies, doan stop there," pitched in Old Knobby, washing down his food with strong, hot tea, which was still far more popular in the West than coffee. "Not only did them red varmints kill our best stud horse, we lost goldang near a dozen top mustangs that ain't never goin' to be rounded up again."

"All that's bad enough," John agreed. "And Will's death the worst of all. That man was solid bedrock. He walked the straight and narrow, but never condemned the rest of us for sinners."

"Speak the truth and shame the devil," Knobby

86

said. "And no slouch with a bronc, neither, was old Will."

"Me, I'm slow to bile," Evan said. "But Will was set to bring his wife and babies out here. Now there's a widder back in Kansas worryin' on how she'll be feedin' two littleuns. I'm slow to bile. But this don't hang right with me. I say them Injins need killin'."

"They aren't here for tribute payment," John agreed. "I should've listened to Knobby in the first place. Don't forget how damn close those renegades came to destroying this house, too. We're lucky we only had to replace the roof. And I *can't* replace the hay they burned. They wiped out nearly half a cutting of new grass. Now I'll have to buy it elsewhere and haul it in."

Corey had not been saying much, lost in worried speculation. Now, hearing a pause after John spoke, Corey said, "I think we should tell Matthew."

All four men started in their chairs when Sarah's cast-iron spider, the three-legged frying pan she set over the kitchen fire, banged loudly off the puncheon floor, missing her foot by inches and spattering buckwheat batter everywhere.

"No!" she said firmly, surprising even herself. "Corey Robinson, I love you like my own son. But you just keep your counsel to yourself. Hiram Steele may be gone, but he made sure Matthew has plenty of enemies left in this valley. This isn't his battle."

"I don't never sass you, Missus Hanchon, you know that. But you know Matthew even better than I know him. *Any* battle you folks have is his

87

battle. If—well, if any harm comes from this, he'll never forgive me for not telling him. And *I* won't forgive me, neither. There's an Arapaho scout at Fort Bates named Coyote. He knows the chief at Matthew's camp, we could send him with a message."

John had risen to put one arm around Sarah, guiding her into his chair. Old Knobby scrambled to clean up the mess on the floor. He and Evan were both scared, seeing Sarah Hanchon so peaked like this. Very rarely did that fine lady ever lose her aplomb.

"Let's make a truce, you two," John said gently. "Honey, Corey is right."

"He's right, yes. But I'm still scared for Matthew, John."

Hanchon nodded. Corey had never seen his employer look so tired and apprehensive. Right when things were really starting to hum along around here.

"I'm scared, too," John said. "So I agree with Sarah. Leave Matthew out of it."

Corey nodded, though reluctantly. "I'll do what you tell me, but it's a mistake. Old Knobby is the only Plains Indian fighter among us. Touch the Sky knows the Comanche tribe. He'd know best how to fight them."

"Corey," Sarah said quietly, but firmly, "I said no."

"Yes'm."

"This time, boy," Old Knobby said, "there's some good sense comin' out your cake-hole. And this hoss'll tell you's all somethin' else with no sugarcoatin'. There's somethin' called the Moccasin Telegraph. The secret ways the Innuns use to spread the word. I swan, she's quick as the white man's copper wires! Might be, ye'll soon be paid a visit by that red son o' yourn, invite or no."

Damn it all, thought Corey.

It just didn't make sense, no matter how a man sliced it. He was no expert on Indians. But having a Cheyenne for his best friend had made him a little more keen to study Indian ways than most men were. And Knobby had told him plenty over the years. Enough to know that this situation with the Comanches made no damn sense at all.

Corey dressed another board with his adze, watching clean, thin pine shavings curl off and flutter in a pile to the ground. This first breaking chute was almost finished. Be a damn shame, he thought, if the Hanchons never got the chance to use it.

Again he thought about these Comanche raiders. What did they want? He knew of the Comanches as an extremely practical tribe, not given to symbolic raids for the purpose of counting coup or taking scalps. They wanted loot: guns, ammo, gold, horses. That, or slaves they could sell to the Comancheros in New Mexico.

So why come this far north from their usual hunting grounds just to harass some paleface ranchers? That attack had been as savage as a meat axe, but they had taken nothing, hadn't even tried. It was as if they had some other purpose in mounting that attack. If—

Corey's thoughts trailed off like smoke in the

wind when he saw them circling about two ridges over: buzzards.

At first he only squinted in idle curiosity. Perhaps they were settling on the remains of some predator's meal. This area was a haven for natural stalkers: coyotes, mountain lions, wolves, foxes, wildcats, owls, hawks, eagles. Carrion birds were not a rarity in Bighorn Valley.

Still . . . that was also right about where John Hanchon's new summer pasture was. The pasture where he had grouped his finest new mustangs under a herd guard.

His freckled forehead wrinkled with worry, Corey lay the next board down and turned toward the yard. Maybe it was best to search out John and tell him?

But no—it was nothing, probably. Why bother John when he was already as busy as a one-legged man at an ass-kicking contest? Corey glanced toward the stone watering trough where his palomino had been tethered. Hell, he could check it out himself.

Corey made a quick trip to the tack room and retrieved his blanket, pad, saddle, and bridle from wooden pegs on the wall. He rigged his horse, checked the latigos, then swung up into leather and whirled his horse around to the north.

He crossed the two timbered ridges in good time, cautiously watching the valley all around him. He spotted one of Hanchon's wranglers well to the south, riding perimeter guard. Then Corey entered the lodgepole pine dotting the far slope of the ridge. He emerged into a pasture of lush bunch grass divided by a freshet.

At first he glanced all around, puzzled. There was no sign of Dez Gillycuddy, the herd guard, *or* of the herd. But the buzzards, they were settling down all over in the pasture. And Christ Almighty, the flies! The air fairly hummed with them.

"What in tarnal hell . . . ?"

The grass was high, well past his horse's knees. So Corey was slow, at first, to notice what the buzzards were descending upon. Then his own horse began to act up as she sniffed something in the wind. She tossed her head, fighting the bit, and Corey saw that her huge, frightened eyes were almost all whites. The palomino tried to turn and run back up the slope behind them, but Corey fought her forward a few more crow-hopping paces.

Far enough to spot something red and glistening in the grass. He looked closer, and recognized the eyeless, castrated corpse as Dez Gillycuddy.

"God-in-whirlwinds!" Corey exclaimed, his blood suddenly reversing course in his veins. He turned away just in time to stop himself from retching. But even as he turned his head, he saw the rest of it: dead horses lying everywhere, some already crawling with carrion birds. John's best stock, all throat-slashed!

And there, in the middle of the killing field, stood a sharpened stick that had been rammed into the ground. Atop it fluttered bits of red and black flannel: the colors of blood and death. Corey knew enough about Indians to know it was a promise that this place, and every man and animal living here, was marked for a hard death.

"Jumpin' Jehosaphat," he told his horse. "Oh,

Katy Christ, we got to warn the others now! Them red devils could swarm down out of these hills any old time they choose."

But even as his frightened pony surged up the ridge, Corey made up his mind. It didn't matter what John and Sarah said. Not now. Corey decided to write that letter to Matthew and send Coyote with it up to the Powder River country. Corey respected the Hanchons, all right. A hell of a lot more, he knew, than he did his own pa. But he was damned if, out of respect for their wishes, he was going to let them and everyone else on this ranch end up like Dez.

"Brother," Little Horse said, no bravado in his tone now. "There it is. I am afraid even to stare up there too long. For surely the Wendigo will steal into our thoughts through our eyes and drive us mad."

Indeed, Little Horse did in fact keep his glance slanted. Before the two braves rose the only accessible slope of Wendigo Mountain. It was precipitous and narrow, rock-strewn, made even more treacherous by loose talus and shale that could trip up even sure-footed mules.

But perhaps the most startling and ghostly feature was the belt of white mist circling the entire mountain about halfway up. It was caused by steam escaping from underground hot springs, then caught in the conflicting wind currents that always buffeted this peak. Once before Touch the Sky had ascended into that blind, deadly cloud—emerging in the rifle sights of a grinning Sis-ki-dee.

Every fiber of his being now resisted going up through that death cloud again—or even setting foot on any part of that slope. But as Arrow Keeper always said: Things are the way they are.

It must get done. Therefore it would get done. Their tribe was called the Fighting Cheyenne because their battles were never over. So Touch the Sky and Little Horse had wasted no time in acting on Little Horse's suggestion. It was crucial to gain information about their enemy's camp, the number of braves Sis-ki-dee now commanded, the extent of their provisions, and perhaps even valuable access to those stolen explosives.

But even though Caleb's camp was located close, on the opposite slope of the Sans Arcs, the two young braves had chosen to stay well hidden. Thus, it was one full sleep, spent in the cover of trees and cutbanks, before they reached the base of Wendigo Mountain.

"From here," Touch the Sky said as they urged their ponies forward, "I see no sentries. But they are not required on the lower slope. The place to have your men would be above the steam cloud."

Little Horse nodded. "And so, emerging, that is the place where we must be all eyes and ears and noses."

At the base of the slope they again halted and swung down from their ponies. Each brave removed four pieces of rawhide from his battle kit and wrapped his pony's hooves, securing them with buckskin fringes. Even though they were unshod, their callused hooves were hard enough to ring on stone.

"We will ride until we reach the cloud," Touch

the Sky said. "Then we muzzle our ponies and hobble them in those rocks to the left of the slope. Put on a second pair of moccasins, brother, for the rest of the climb is on foot. Here, give me your hand."

Puzzled, Little Horse did as his friend directed. Touch the Sky guided the warrior's fingers to the grizzly claws dangling around his neck.

"Look at me," he said somewhat sharply to Little Horse. When his friend had done this, Touch the Sky added, "Do you recognize the object you are now touching?"

"Brother, how could I not? Am I as stupid as Swift Canoe? It is the fine present Honey Eater made for your marriage gift."

"Fine, indeed. But know this. Arrow Keeper appeared to her in a dream and told her to make it."

Little Horse was solemn and silent for at least ten heartbeats after this revelation.

"Do you understand," Touch the Sky persisted, "why I am having you touch it?"

Little Horse nodded.

"Good. Here." Touch the Sky reached up and untied the leather cord threaded through the two sets of claws. "Here. Take one and tie it around your neck. You touched it while I wore it, now you will wear it. May the High Holy Ones ride with us."

"Ha-ho, ha-ho," Little Horse said in Cheyenne, accepting it. "Thank you. If we must fall, brother, land on Blackfoot bones!"

With those simple words, the two warriors did not defeat their fear. But they had looked it in the eye and nodded to it, as equals will. Now they headed up the slope of the only hell their people believed in.

Chapter Nine

Touch the Sky's confidence that no sentries had been placed on the slope eroded as they closed the distance to the peak of Wendigo Mountain.

He looked for death at every step upward gained by his strong little chestnut. The slope was steep and treacherous, with sheer cliffs falling away close at hand on both sides—and at the bottom of the cliffs, sharp basalt turrets capable of skewering a man through like raw meat on a spit. This left the two Indians little time for careful observation of the many excellent ambush spots just above on both sides of the rough trail.

More than once the superior training of their ponies, as well as the animals' mountain blood and instincts, saved both riders from death or serious injury. Even as a piece of loose shale cost a pony its footing on one leg, it nimbly danced or crow-hopped to a more secure position.

Since the Cheyenne braves were thus deprived of their eyes, they maintained absolute silence and listened closely for any sounds that did not belong to the natural scheme of things. They paused often so that Little Horse could sample the air closely with his nose: the stout warrior had trained his sense of smell to detect many of the odors animals could detect. Through patience and experience, Touch the Sky too had sharpened his sense of smell. He could sometimes sniff a large group of enemy horses at up to a hundred paces away. At night, he could locate bodies of water by their distinctive smell.

But fear sweat had a distinctive smell, too: like sharp, sheared copper, the odor of fresh blood. And Touch the Sky smelled it coming off him and his friend as they inched closer and closer to that cingulum of white mist circling the mountain.

The wind howled nonstop, only now and then rising to a high-pitched keening that struck cold terror in both youths' hearts. How easy it was to believe, hearing that heart-rending, plaintive wailing, that it was indeed the cry of their long-lost Cheyenne ancestors who leaped off that cliff to avoid death by torture.

The chestnut's powerful haunches and muscle-corded chest were equal to the slope. Even so, the unsure footing strained their animals, and more often now they stopped to blow. When they did, both braves stared hard above. But all seemed deserted, as it should be on this unholy mountain.

At one point Little Horse nudged his pony close

and said low in his comrade's ear, "Brother, a thing troubles me."

"Have you swallowed a bone, Cheyenne? Speak it."

"Only this. Could we be wrong, and violating this place needlessly? We have no proof we can place in our sashes that our enemy is camped up there. We are well up the trail now. If he is up there, why would there not at least be a few sharp-shooters?"

Touch the Sky could tell, from the worried set of Little Horse's lips, that he already had guessed the answer to this question.

"Perhaps," Touch the Sky replied, "because Sis-ki-dee is so confident his force is beyond any harm up there."

Little Horse nodded. Then, because there was no other place for this grim observation to take them but the grave, Little Horse added a nervy grin. "Brother, we can make misery any place we go! Let these cricket-eating Blackfoot intruders discover the price of Cheyenne pride!"

But despite his friend's bravado, Touch the Sky knew that the ring of warm mist was drawing closer. Soon, brave talk would be nothing, and they would discover the depths of their courage in action, not hollow words.

As agreed, just shy of the roiling clouds of steam they dismounted and led their ponies into a little shelter of rocks. They hobbled them, then again checked their weapons. And now began the truly unnerving stretch of their climb.

Entering the steamy mist was like walking into

dream time and dream space. The sun was muted to a dull saffron glow, objects lost their shape and definition and became menacing forms about to leap on them. Sounds, oddly distorted by the wet air, lost their physical logic: Touch the Sky could not distinguish near from far, nor determine the direction from which a noise came.

More than once, as their feet loosed a rock or the wind rustled a scrawny clump of spindle tree, the two braves went flat on the ground, their weapons trained on absolutely nothing but their own fear. But eventually, just when the tension threatened to become unbearable, the swirling clouds of steam began to dissipate. They were about to emerge from this ascent through the fog of death.

Using hand signals and nods, they adhered to their original plan: instead of emerging on the trail, each went wide to one side, crowding the sheer cliffs. Thus Touch the Sky and Little Horse emerged for a clear view of the pinnacle of Wendigo Mountain.

Touch the Sky's jaw went slack with surprise.

"Brother," he said quietly from the shelter of a little pile of scree, "tell me I do not see it."

Little Horse swallowed hard to find his voice. "You see it, buck," he assured his friend. "Unless, together, we have gone crazy by thunder. Now we know why they have not bothered to protect the slope. The porcupine sleeps where it will."

"Yes. As does the skunk."

Stretching out above them, nearly to the very peak of the mountain, was a formidably constructed bastion. Already, there were enough wickiups and dugouts to rival the huge Pawnee camp on the Republican River. At least fifty fine mustangs had been grouped in a rope corral. Blackfoot braves dotted the area.

"Brother," Little Horse said, "there are more Blackfoot warriors present than a sane man would like to face. Still, do you notice a thing? There are far more shelters than required for this many men."

Touch the Sky's lips formed their grim, determined slit. "Straight words, buck. There are more men. Either in the area now or coming."

"This is no temporary camp," Little Horse said. "Look there! Sturdy meat racks. And over there— they have constructed a sweat lodge. No Indian builds such things in a trail camp."

Both braves were stunned by the implications of this sight. This amounted to having a major enemy tribe establish its homeland on the edge of Cheyenne hunting grounds.

"Truly," Touch the Sky said grimly, "it could not have come at a worse time. Our tribe is now too divided against itself to fight a common enemy. We must try—"

"Maiyun help us now," Little Horse suddenly muttered, cutting his friend off. "Brother, it is my turn to check my eyes. Do you see them, too, or have I eaten peyote?"

Little Horse nodded toward a jacal or brush shanty in the center of this new bastion. Three braves were just then emerging into plain view.

Touch the Sky looked at their faces, and the shock of recognition was instant. Fear robbed him of his next breath.

Grimly, he nodded. "I see them, brother. But I would tear every feather from my best bonnet to be wrong. It matters not if our tribe is ready for this battle—when it comes, we will either have to win it or it will be the end of the Cheyenne Nation."

The shock of it still numbed Touch the Sky's face as he watched the trio walk slowly through camp, deep in some conversation. For there walked his three worst enemies in all the world. A warrior's nightmare had finally come true: the Comanche terror Big Tree had made common cause with the Blackfoot butcher Sis-ki-dee. And to ensure the eventual destruction of Caleb Riley and the Cheyenne people who stayed loyal to the Arrows, there stood the ambitious traitor Wolf Who Hunts Smiling.

But Touch the Sky had learned to trust his instincts more, to look at things also with the shaman eye. The apparent shape of a thing, Arrow Keeper had taught him, was not always its substance. This huge camp going up—it did indeed portend serious trouble for Gray Thunder's Powder River *Shaiyena*. Just as it was already proving disastrous for Caleb Riley's camp.

Still, some other, more immediate danger loomed. The shape of things did not fit Touch the Sky's inner sense of them; there existed a disharmony between appearances and realities. He must quickly read the true shapes written in the sand, or some horrible disaster would befall him—or worse, someone he loved.

Touch the Sky had seen enough. There was no sign of the stolen explosives, but this dangerous

climb was justified. Now it was time to return to
Caleb Riley's camp and find out what Tangle Hair
and Two Twists might have learned.

He gripped his friend's shoulder hard, then
rolled his head back toward the slope. Little Horse
nodded, casting one last, apprehensive glance toward the deadly trio above them. A moment later,
silent as gliding shadows, the two Cheyenne intruders were gone.

"Aunt?"

Honey Eater, deeply preoccupied, was slow to
respond to little Laughing Brook. "Hmm? What is
it, child?"

Shortly after the spring melt, Gray Thunder's
tribe had received its annual consignment of trade
goods from Caleb Riley, a peace price for hauling
his ore out over their hunting grounds. These
goods included bolts of new calico and linsey-
woolsey, and now Honey Eater was showing her
niece how to make the intricate and narrow Cheyenne rickrack braiding envied throughout the
Plains.

"Why has Medicine Flute been staring at you so
long?"

Honey Eater's face went cold, but she was smart
enough not to glance up. Keeping her tone casual,
continuing her work, she said, "What do you
mean, sweet love? Where is he? No, don't point,
child. Just tell me. And here, watch me work, silly!
I'm not doing this for my health, I want you to
learn it."

"He's over by the dance lodge. He won't stop
staring at you. He's staring because you're so

pretty. But I don't like him."

Laughing Brook had only six winters behind her, but everyone agreed she was a true prodigy. Pretty and smart, just like her aunt. Also like Honey Eater, she had taken to braiding white columbine in her hair. Now her face was defiant as she stared toward Medicine Flute.

"Why don't you like him, sweet?"

"His music scares me. When he blows on that bone, the little babies cry. I don't like him. When— here he comes, Aunt!"

"Shh, *look* at my hands, child! See? See how I pulled the colored threads over the—"

A harsh bark of laughter cut into Honey Eater's desperate patter.

"No more ruses, pretty Honey Eater," Medicine Flute told her. "My ears hear worms digging, and my eyes see all around Touch the Sky's."

Medicine Flute suddenly bent close to Laughing Brook, his face only inches from hers. She went pale as moonstone.

"I don't like you, either," he told her bluntly, shocking Honey Eater immobile, it was so unexpected. "But I have magic powers, little one. And I promise you: soon, when you are asleep in the night, I am sending Rawhead and Bloody Bones to your tipi!"

Rawhead and Bloody Bones were the most feared bogeys among Cheyenne little ones. Such a threat, coming from an adult like Medicine Flute, carried the weight of a death sentence. In a heartbeat, Laughing Brook was howling with uncontrollable terror, choking with powerful sobs that wracked her entire body.

Honey Eater's rage was instant, as was her need to comfort this terrified child. All of an instant she threw down her work, rose, and slapped Medicine Flute so hard it left his skull ringing.

"You are no man!" she spat at him as she scooped her sobbing niece into her arms and made the age-old comforting sounds that men's cruelty has forced women to learn. "And yet, you are lower than any animal, for animals are not cruel!"

Anger flared up in Medicine Flute. Never had he known of a Cheyenne woman to strike a man! But even as he was on the feather edge of knocking the child from her arms, he drew up short. For there, watching him from the entrance of the Bow String lodge, was Spotted Tail. Touch the Sky's lick-spittles were always guarding Honey Eater.

So instead, as Laughing Brook slowly quieted, he only waited until Honey Eater met his eye.

"I will mark this day and the grievous insult you paid me. The time is coming, sooner than your pride will admit, when your tall licker of white crotches will feed maggots. Think carefully. You can change your loyalties—and your tipi—now while there is still time. But this place hears what I say. When his time comes, he will not cross over alone. All his followers will go with him."

Chapter Ten

The Arapaho scout named Coyote was paid ten white man's dollars every month—two shiny gold half-eagles—for doing what he used to do every day for nothing: keep his eyes out for trouble.

The huge area he covered was bound by the Missouri River to the east, the old Bent's Fort near the Smoky Hills to the south, the Canadian River to the west, and the Black Hills to the north. Thus, he was not derelict in his duties when he rode north to the upcountry of the Powder with Corey's letter for Touch the Sky.

But Coyote encountered a Cheyenne hunting party along the way and shared a pipe of good paleface tobacco with them. Thus it was he learned that Touch the Sky would instead be found at the mining camp in the Sans Arcs. He was waiting when the tall brave and his friend Little Horse rode in with their disturbing news about Wendigo Mountain.

For a long time Touch the Sky held the folded-over sheet of foolscap without reading it. His heart was heavy with dread.

Caleb, Little Horse, and the others had stepped back, letting their friend have his moment of solitude. Touch the Sky looked at them.

"Corey wouldn't send word," he told them, "unless it was very serious. He shares this trait with the red man—he is not one for idle chatter."

With that, Touch the Sky opened the folded sheet and read the brief note printed in painfully neat, hopelessly misspelled capital letters. For a long time, after he finished reading it, his face went warm and numb. When he looked at his friends again, he was surprised by the shock in their faces. Was the horror of it that clear in his own face?

"The game is clear to me now," he announced. "They have caught me in a bluecoat pincer's movement. This time, Wolf Who Hunts Smiling has outdone himself. For even as Sis-ki-dee and his renegades terrorize this camp, Big Tree and his are out to destroy my white parents in Bighorn Falls."

He spoke first in English, then Cheyenne. Caleb's face fell, but Little Horse showed little surprise, only nodding. Now it all made sense to him, too.

They were all standing near the pile of wrangled metal from which Ernie's unrecognizable remains had been removed for burial. By Caleb's strict order, all women and children were restricted to their homes except for emergencies. Now, armed men patrolled the camp streets and the outlying region.

Not surprisingly, it was the swaggering Two Twists who first rallied them after this fresh bad news.

"No time for womanly hand-wringing, bucks! If Comanche blood be rain, let us ride south and cause a flash flood!"

Many of the miners glanced over in nervous surprise when the young Indian thrust his lance up and yipped a Cheyenne war cry. But though he was the youngest warrior present, all of his comrades knew this was not blustery talk. The independent spirit that caused him to wear a double braid also made him a warrior second to none. When all seemed lost, Two Twists would rally his comrades to victory through sheer audacity and courage. No one was very surprised at this, considering that he learned the Warrior Way from Touch the Sky and Little Horse.

"Drink water for your blood thirst," Touch the Sky scolded him. "This is no time to take the enemy's bait. For bait it is. They will kill my parents, surely. Comanches do not scruple to kill their own wives and children. But their true objective is this mining camp. If we all ride down now like birds fleeing in front of a storm, we will dance to their cadence."

Two Twists did not like something here. He frowned, his young face perplexed. "You who risked your life to save my parents will now let your own die?"

"Buck," Little Horse said quietly, "I would kill a

106

stranger for saying that to our shaman."

"Let it alone," Touch the Sky said quietly, pouring oil on the waters. "Two Twists did not intend disrespect. No, double braid with the careless mouth, I do not intend to let my parents die. I am leaving Little Horse and Tangle Hair here with Caleb. And as for me, I am riding to Bighorn Falls, with the intention of returning as quickly as possible. I intend to fight Big Tree there, and I mean to take you with me. Now stop gawking and tend to your battle rig, and if you cry for your mother I will dress you in a shawl."

Touch the Sky had acted so quickly and decisively because young Two Twists was right: There was no time for womanly hand-wringing. Even now his parents were under the gun, threatened by a renegade second to none for cruelty and battle savvy.

So he and Two Twists wasted no time. They stuffed their legging sashes with pemmican, accepted a generous ration of powder and ball from Caleb, then pointed their bridles south toward Bighorn Falls.

Touch the Sky knew the situation here in the Sans Arcs was desperate. But in leaving Little Horse behind, he truly believed he had left his equal and the best man he could have chosen. As for Tangle Hair, he was not given to boasting as many Indians were. But he fought like ten braves. Too, Caleb had turned into a damn good frontiersman, and most of his men had sand in them. No, Touch the Sky told himself—it was his white parents who were in more dire straits right now, for Big Tree was making their lives a hurting place.

He and Two Twists had just debouched from a deep cutbank in the Sans Arc foothills when Touch the Sky spotted them: two Blackfoot braves standing on the embankment of Beaver Creek.

"Look," Two Twists said after his companion pointed them out, "why are they aiming their rifles at the dam? They cannot possibly hurt it with bullets."

Indeed, the two braves were just then drawing beads on a crude mud dam which pick-and-shovel miners had originally built to expose the gold-bearing gravel here. But when the spring runoff was copious, as it was now, the dam served a second purpose: It kept the creek from flooding the railroad spur built just below it in the valley.

"No," Touch the Sky agreed even as one of the braves fired his weapon, "bullets could not hurt that dam. But something else might. Little brother, raise the war cry now and make your pony fly! We must rout those warriors."

"Hi-ya! Hii-*ya!*"

Uttering their shrill, yipping war cry, the two braves jabbed heels into their ponies' flanks and tore across the valley. Touch the Sky speared his Sharps from its buckskin scabbard and snapped off a round, not bothering to aim at this distance, only wanting to frighten the Blackfoot braves.

This they accomplished. The two braves raised their weapons to defend themselves. Then, one of them pointed—as if recognizing this tall, broad-shouldered Cheyenne brave. A moment later they scrambled up the embankment, leaped on their ponies, and escaped into the lodgepole pine.

When Two Twists started to give chase, Touch the Sky halted him with a shouted command. "Never mind glory, buck! Those cricket eaters were not shooting for sport. Stay here with the ponies and be sure those two do not return to shoot us in the back."

"What are you doing?" Two Twists demanded when Touch the Sky hobbled his own mount and kicked his moccasins off in the grass and untied his legging sash. But Touch the Sky only ignored him, plunging into the runoff-swollen creek.

Sometimes walking, sometimes swimming when the current swept his feet out from under him, Touch the Sky began a quick examination of the crude dam. He found it almost immediately: A canvas-covered object about the size and shape of a seat cushion. It had been placed into a crack in the face of the dam, much of it still exposed.

Touch the Sky could read the warning without touching the device: NITROGLYCERIN GEL. CAUTION, EXTREMELY VOLATILE. HANDLE CAREFULLY. EXCESSIVE HEAT OR SHARP, CONCUSSIVE CONTACT WILL DETONATE.

He had guessed correctly. The two braves meant to set it off with a bullet, thus flooding the tracks so Caleb couldn't use them even when he brought in his replacement locomotive. Clearly, if he left it here, they'd soon be back to finish the job. Best to remove it and detonate it in a harmless spot, rendering the charge useless to them.

Reluctantly, nervous sweat beading on his forehead, Touch the Sky braced his leg muscles

Judd Cole

against the current and carefully gripped the nitro gel. Praying to Maiyun that he wouldn't lose his footing in the process, he managed to get it back to shore.

"Brother, what manner of thing is this?" Two Twists demanded.

Touch the Sky explained, emphasizing its dangerously volatile nature. But as he was searching for a place to detonate it, another thought occurred to him: Considering the fight that he and Two Twists were about to face, it might be foolish to waste such a powerful weapon. True, the thought of carrying it on horseback made Touch the Sky's skin go clammy. But so did the thought of Comanches terrorizing his parents.

"Two Twists," he said, his tone joking, "ride well back from me, buck, for I am taking this with me. If it detonates, pick my feathers out of the treetops and give them to my widow."

His warning was unnecessary, for already Two Twists was scrambling away from him, his eyes huge. It was not fear of death, but fear of this unknown, unclean, white man's way of dying, that struck him with awe.

"Brother," he said uncertainly, "is this the warrior or the shaman making this decision?"

"The shaman."

Two Twists nodded, somewhat reassured. "Then it will kill Comanches," he said confidently. Perhaps it was a point of honor with him, or a vote of confidence in his shaman. But for the rest of the journey Two Twists refused to ride further than an arm's length from his companion.

*   *   *

"It ain't you, Mr. Hanchon," said a lanky wrangler named Reno Sloan. "Why, hell! You and your wife are the best folks I ever rode for. But me, I got my belly full of fightin' under Old Fuss and Feathers when we rode into Mexico City back in '49. And these Comanches, they make the Mexer army look like school girls."

"No apologies needed, Reno," John Hanchon assured him. The rancher opened a tin box and counted out a stack of silver dollars. "You didn't sign on to fight Indians. There's a month's wages and a few dollars extra."

Reno Sloan, looking miserable, swooped the money into his pocket and left the house, boot heels thudding on the puncheon floor.

"Well," Evan Blackford said, "that's three more've quit and pulled up stakes. With Will and Dez both kilt, that makes five hands short. Lose any more, I swan this holler will be nigh empty of white men."

The foreman fell silent and, along with Old Knobby and Corey, followed John as he went out into the main yard. Hanchon gazed out toward the summer pasture, where even now his best horses were fertilizing the very grass they were supposed to be eating.

"Those horses were already sold," he muttered to no one in particular. "I already spent the money. First it was my mercantile store they took, now I'm fighting again to save this place. A man doesn't bust his hump just for the love of sweat. I been tryin' to put by against the future, mainly for Sarah's sake. But the way things look now, she'll be taking in washing long after I'm planted."

"They ain't whupped us yet," Old Knobby said defiantly.

"Not by half," Corey pitched in.

"No, not yet," John said wearily, glancing out at the ridges surrounding them. "They're having a high-old time just picking us off one by one. Colonel Lyman at the fort claims he's sent a request to his superiors up in Dakota, seeking permission to look into the matter. By the time the Army gets off its duff, this place'll be a memory."

"Hell," Evan's nervous voice suddenly cut in, "check your loads, gents. Here's two savages ridin' in! See 'em yonder, just now comin' down the ridge?"

They all stared out toward the spot where Evan pointed.

"Them ain't Comanche," Old Knobby said after staring at the new arrivals. "And they're flyin' a peace flag."

"Lower your muzzle," Corey told John, speaking up boldly now. "That's your son, Mr. Hanchon. I defied you and sent for him."

"Good for you, boy," Knobby muttered.

But if John Hanchon was angry at Corey's disobedience, the sight of his adopted son returning home overcame it.

"Sarah!" he shouted back toward the house. "Better come on outside, we got company you'll want to meet."

The kitchen door swung open and Sarah emerged into the coppery late-afternoon sunshine, wiping her hands on a clean apron. "Sakes and saints," she complained, "I'm hardly ready for company. Why didn't you. . . ."

Her voice trailed off when she spotted the two riders nearing the house. At first her face went blank, then curious. In a moment the curiosity deepened to a certainty. As the two riders trotted into the yard, tears spilled past Sarah's eyelashes.

The two young Cheyennes halted their exotically marked and rigged mustangs. John and Sarah had their arms around their son even before he slid to the ground. The other Indian, the younger one with twin braids, Knobby noticed, sat his pony, looking confused and unsure as these whites converged on his friend.

"Matthew," Sarah managed when she could speak past the tight lump in her throat. "Son, you shouldn't have come here. But sweet heart of Jesus, I'm so happy to see you!"

"Your Ma's right," John said gruffly. "You shouldn't be here."

"From the looks of all those dead horses I saw just now as we were riding in," Touch the Sky replied, "you can use all the help you can get."

"*There*'s a home truth," Knobby said, grinning like a happy baby as he studied his young friend. "Sprout, you've picked up a few more battle scars since this child last seed ye."

With one arm still around his mother, Touch the Sky violated Indian custom by accepting the hand Knobby shoved at him to shake. But even as he reached out, there was a fast fwipping sound and a white-hot wire of pain creased Touch the Sky's arm.

From long battle experience, he recognized it immediately. But at the same moment he felt his mother suddenly go limp and heavy on his arm.

113

"Jee-zuz jumpin' Christ!" Old Knobby shouted.

A startled shout emerged from John's throat. He and his son moved at the same moment. But nobody was quick enough to catch her when Sarah Hanchon collapsed to the ground, a Comanche arrow protruding from her back.

Chapter Eleven

"Even now," Wolf Who Hunts Smiling gloated, "Big Tree is down in Bighorn Falls, doing the hurt dance on White Man Runs Him and his paleface clan. Our noble red man took the bait, just as I said he would. Soon Caleb Riley's camp and everything in it will be ours."

He, Sis-ki-dee, and Sis-ki-dee's favorite lackey, Scalp Cane, stood beside one of the stolen Requa rifle batteries that had just been situated, during the previous night, behind the rimrock overlooking the mining camp. Its 25 barrels were arranged horizontally on a light frame that allowed them to be aimed and fired as one. Each barrel would spit seven rounds per minute for a total of 125 shots.

"Two more of these," Sis-ki-dee told Wolf Who Hunts Smiling, "have been dragged into place on those ridges to the west. My men hid them well

115

behind deadfalls. When the time comes to take that camp, we will rain lead on them."

"I have ears for this." Wolf Who Hunts Smiling's lupine grin divided his face. On that first day, when Sis-ki-dee and Big Tree had both combined their warriors back on Wendigo Mountain, the sight had been formidable. But what would that mountain-top fortress be like once a hundred or so Cheyenne braves joined his new Renegade Nation? The time was coming, and soon. It required only the death of Touch the Sky to assure a virtual red kingdom under the control of Wolf Who Hunts Smiling. And the riches of that camp below to help sustain it.

But then his grin wavered as he thought of something else.

"Know this, Contrary Warrior," he added. "We have successfully lured our enemy to the south, true. And we have powerful bluecoat weapons on our side. But Caleb Riley has grown some hard bark on him since coming out here with green velvet on his antlers.

"He will not show the white feather and flee like some cowardly Ponca. And never forget that White Man Runs Him left Little Horse and Tangle Hair behind. Respect both of them, Red Peril. Neither brave plans to die in his tipi."

"About this Tangle Hair I can say nothing. But I and my men have tried our best to kill this Little Horse," Sis-ki-dee admitted. "Yet, still he walks the earth. And now I have a caution for you. When next you see Big Tree, warn him. For the tall bear caller has laid hands on one of our explosives.

Scalp Cane here swears it is gone. I fear he took it south with him."

"He did," Scalp Cane threw in. "No one else could have it."

This news angered Wolf Who Hunts Smiling. He glowered at Scalp Cane. "Your men lack the brains of a rabbit! *That* one is danger enough without giving him more power."

"So is that explosive dangerous?" Sis-ki-dee said, grinning. "He may yet kill himself with it."

"Not that one. He has stayed alive by avoiding mistakes the way horses avoid bears or mules snakes. However, tell me bucks. When am *I* ever idle? Touch the Sky will surely ride north again to meet with his friends.

"I, too, am riding between this place and Big-horn Falls to serve as a courier between you and Big Tree. Before our enemy rode south, I managed to carve a notch in one of his pony's hooves. I will be watching for that mark. And when I cut sign on him, I will also find Touch the Sky and kill him."

"Familiar words," Sis-ki-dee said. "Had I a Spanish pistoreen for each time you foretold his death, I would be wealthy. But I wish you well, wily Wolf. And certainly, never before has he had death breathing on him from so many directions. Big Tree sports with him to the south. I sport with him to the north. You turn his life dangerous in between. Truly he is trapped between the sap and the bark."

"Scalp Cane," Wolf Who Hunts Smiling snapped. "Are you a fool? They have sentries stationed below and on horseback. Get back behind cover."

The Blackfoot had broken cover to examine some marks carved high up in a pine tree. He did as the Cheyenne ordered. But he remarked, his tone worried, "A silvertip has made its territorial mark there. This is the fourth tree I have seen thus marked in this area. Despite so many humans below, grizzlies live in this area."

"Buck," Sis-ki-dee teased his lick-spittle, "you play the worried squaw like this because you have heard too many tales about the mighty Bear Caller!"

As Sis-ki-dee said this, he watched the camp below in its teacup-shaped hollow halfway up the mountain. At this height, the human beings below resembled little more than bugs. But it was clear that no work was going forward, and that most of the bugs visible in camp were in fact heavily armed men on sentry duty.

Occasionally, however, during the past few sleeps, two women had appeared briefly on the street, accompanied by Riley himself. Sis-ki-dee studied the camp often and knew the routine. They would emerge from one of the lodges and cross through the camp streets to another lodge set behind the others. Here, water from a gravity cistern flowed down for bathing.

It would be virtually impossible to attack that lodge through the heavily armed camp. However, two crazy-brave warriors might swoop down the steep mountain behind it. A risk, surely. But these two women struck fire in his loins. They justified the risk, as did his need to live on the feather edge of danger.

"What are you thinking?" Wolf Who Hunts Smiling demanded, watching the Contrary Warrior's face and not liking what he read there.

Sis-ki-dee threw back his head and roared with scornful laughter. "Only this, buck. My men are becoming hard to control for lack of women. A man is like a volcano. If he does not relieve the pressure, he will explode. Perhaps soon, after Scalp Cane and I have relieved our own pressure first, we will have a present for the men."

"I tell you again," Sarah Hanchon insisted, "I'm perfectly fine. And John, I will *not* let that so-called doctor from town touch me! Not only does he charge a dollar a mile for house calls, all he has with him is castor oil and calomel. Holly Nearhood suffered from catarrh and made the mistake of going to him. He purged the poor thing until she nearly died."

Despite the fact that she lay flat on her stomach, Sarah's words were loud and clear to the circle of nervous men standing awkwardly around the feather bed set up for her in the parlor.

"She doan need no sawbones," Knobby declared. "I snapped that arrow off clean, and the point come out the front without strikin' vitals. Jist let her rest a spell, make sure it knits right."

The men—John Hanchon, Old Knobby, Evan Blackford, Corey, Touch the Sky, and Two Twists—moved back out into the yard.

"I kallate that arrow come at least five-hundred yards," Knobby said, his voice subdued at the thought of such marksmanship.

Touch the Sky, his face grim, still held part of the broken shaft. Without a word he held it out to Two Twists and showed him the peculiar notches near the fletching.

"Do you recognize it, buck?" he said in Cheyenne.

Two Twists nodded. "Big Tree. It is the same mark we found on the long arrow he shot through you in your sleep. It was Big Tree who almost sent your mother under."

Touch the Sky nodded and turned to the others, switching to English.

"All of you know the Comanche tribe. They are no braves to fool with. But this one we are up against now would frighten every devil out of the white man's hell. He's also smart as a steel trap. His name is Big Tree, and I tell you now. It is no accident that he has come here. He was sent to lure me out of the Sans Arcs while his new partner in terror destroys Caleb Riley's mining camp."

"He shot a woman in the back," John said. "I don't credit my own eyes."

"Them heathen sonsabitches need to meet the hemp committee," Evan averred. "And the one that aired Sarah needs to taste a blacksnake whip on his hide first."

"Pee doodles!" Knobby spat. "A Comanch doan see no difference between man, woman, nor child when it comes to killin'. No need to git all wrathy and go out there with short irons blazin'. Best to stay frosty and shoot plumb. Elsewise, we'll *all* be wearin' one a them Indian haircuts."

"Shoot plumb at what?" John demanded, frustration heavy in his voice. "Jesus God! By the time a man gets his piece settled in his shoulder, they're out of range."

Touch the Sky had fallen silent again while the others debated. For now, since understanding this new scheme hatched by Wolf Who Hunts Smiling, the tall Cheyenne also had a clearer understanding of Arrow Keeper's dream warning: *You must ride with magic on one flank, white man's cunning on the other.*

"Pa's right," he said. "They won't give us much to shoot at. And a Comanche has no fear about attacking at night. Each strike is going to get a little bolder, bring them a little closer to the house. Shooting at them won't be enough."

"The hell else *can* we do?" Corey demanded. "Throw rocks at 'em?"

Touch the Sky shook his head. None of this was the style of fighting preferred by a Plains warrior. Forting up from a fixed position was a white man's custom that frightened Indians. They would rather skirmish from horseback, changing locations frequently. But this time there was nothing else for it—thus Arrow Keeper's dream warning.

"No, we don't throw rocks. We erect defenses designed to cripple their chief advantage—their horses."

Knobby listened thoughtfully to all of this, digging at a tick in his beard. John still looked unconvinced, but the old trapper began to nod agreement. "I take your drift. Separate a Comanch from his hoss, he's gone beaver."

Touch the Sky nodded.

"What kind of defenses?" Corey said.

"Breastworks," Old Knobby responded promptly. "Pointed stakes painted black, set out after dark so they can't spot 'em aforehand. We can dig rifle pits so's they can't spot *us*, neither."

"Post holes will trip their horses," John added, starting to pick up on the vague sense of hope now being generated. "And we can dig firebreaks."

"How?" demanded Evan. "Laws! The boys are afeared to poke their noses out the bunkhouse. Them red bastards—beg pardon, Matthew, no offense to you or your pard—can pick a body off without leavin' them ridges yonder."

"They can during the day," Touch the Sky agreed. "So it'll get done tonight after sundown. It'll still be dangerous because they might attack at night. But it's either that or Pa might as well torch this place now."

While Touch the Sky translated for Two Twists, the other four men discussed the tall Cheyenne's plan. Finally, all agreed they could come up with nothing better. But Touch the Sky knew he would not be needed to do this work tonight: Now that he had learned the situation here in Bighorn Falls and knew that a plan was in place, he must ride hard and fast to the Sans Arcs to counsel with Little Horse and Tangle Hair.

He recalled something else. In the confusion of arrival and the wounding of his mother, he had forgotten about the nitro gel in his kit. He reminded himself to store it in a safe place—and to be very careful about where he employed it. In this battle that was looming, one poorly placed defense could cost them the victory—and their lives.

* * *

"It is quiet, brother," Little Horse said. "But then, so is a dead man."

He and Tangle Hair had taken on the dangerous task of serving as mounted sentries around the perimeter of the mining camp. Now they were halted above a talus slope overlooking the west side of the camp, letting their ponies drink from a natural sink formed by rocks trapping rain water.

The center of camp lay far below them. From here it seemed well protected, at least once you entered the camp proper. But out here, Little Horse knew, it was Sis-ki-dee's game to name. The white miners did not lack courage and fortitude. But they did not have the experience with this rugged terrain that Sis-ki-dee and his marauders possessed.

Again, as he had often lately, Little Horse raised a finger tip to the grizzly claw Touch the Sky gave him to wear. He was worried about his friend, as any brave would worry when Big Tree was in the mix. But more than anything, Little Horse wished Touch the Sky would return north to help them. Little Horse was not afraid to die. Against Sis-ki-dee and Wolf Who Hunts Smiling, however, it was only natural to want a warrior—and a shaman—of Touch the Sky's prowess.

Little Horse abruptly frowned.

"What is it, buck?" Tangle Hair said.

Little Horse nodded toward the ridge below the talus slope. "I thought I saw something glint down there. Something shiny."

"Something," prompted Tangle Horse, "like the pieces of silver in Sis-ki-dee's Mexican saddle?"

"As you say, brave."

Tangle Hair's voice went grim. "Well, notice something else. Look to the west end of camp."

The keen-eyed Little Horse did look. Caleb was escorting Kristen Steele and his wife Woman Dress to the bathing lodge.

Little Horse again glanced below—long enough to realize that the spot where he thought he saw the flash was right behind the bathing lodge. And then he understood what was about to happen.

"Tangle Hair! This talus below us is dangerous. But buck, ride like the wind, now comes bloody sport!"

Even as the two Cheyennes heeled their ponies into motion, Little Horse saw them break out from cover below: the Contrary Warrior and one other Blackfoot, both on horseback.

At first, the desperate Little Horse saw no hope of getting down there in time—especially when his pony lost her footing on the long talus slope and went down. Yet that misfortune proved a blessing. Both Cheyenne ponies fell, sliding fast but harmlessly down the steep slope until they hit solid ground again. The game little mustangs came up running, and all of a sudden a desperate race was on.

The trio below were alerted to danger and had stopped in the street before the lodge. With a dexterity and accuracy that stunned Little Horse, Siski-dee raised his North & Savage and blasted off a round. Little Horse's stomach turned over when he saw Caleb smash to the ground.

Instead of running for shelter, both women instantly dropped over Caleb to help him. Now Little Horse and Tangle Hair pounded down from the right, Sis-ki-dee and his companion from the left. Their ponies crashed through saplings and shrubs, stumbled over loose boulders, leaped fallen logs.

It's no use, Little Horse thought desperately. *It's no use! We can't beat them!*

Unconscious that he was doing it, Little Horse raised his hand to the grizzly claw around his neck.

He was forced to suddenly hang on for dear life as his mustang abruptly seemed to sprout wings, as did Tangle Hair's. They surged forward, and Little Horse reached out just as Tangle Hair did, leaning low from their ponies. Little Horse caught up Kristen, and Tangle Hair lifted Woman Dress, only heartbeats before the two Blackfoot renegades would have.

A moment later Caleb, wounded but wearing a war face, struggled to his knees and speared the Smith & Wesson from its holster. A hail of lead escorted the Blackfoot intruders back into the rimland.

Chapter Twelve

"Aunt, this is madness in our own camp!"

Honey Eater threw down the wild onion she was slicing. With Touch the Sky gone, she now took her meals with the widowed Sharp Nosed Woman. The hunters had ridden in before sunset with some fine antelope and a plump doe. Because the Cheyenne meat-distribution always favored the elderly, poor, and widowed, Sharp Nosed Woman had received some fine loin meat and a tasty bit of brain, which she promptly boiled with rosehips.

"Niece, lower your voice," Sharp Nosed Woman cautioned her, keeping her own tone quiet by example. "You promised we might have a peaceful meal this night. I—"

"Is my husband enjoying a peaceful meal? Are Little Horse and Tangle Hair and Two Twists?

Aunt, you shame me finally! Do you know that little Laughing Brook has not once lived up to her name since that bone-blowing monster Medicine Flute terrified her? I assure you, *she* will not enjoy a peaceful meal this evening!"

"Honey Eater, you are a Cheyenne woman, not a war leader! This behavior—"

"This behavior, Aunt, is consistent with a great chief's teachings that nothing must come before the sacred honor of our Medicine Arrows. My father was that great chief, and now my husband is the Keeper of our Arrows!"

"Niece, I swear before Maiyun, if you do not lower your voice, I will borrow a gun from one of the soldiers and shoot you! I know perfectly well who your father was. And truly, breathes there a Cheyenne in camp who cannot name your husband? Only those with a dug in their mouth.

"But Honey Eater, take reason firmly by the tail before you regret your rash conduct. Do you see how things are? Touch the Sky told this tribe he was riding into the Sans Arcs to protect our interests. Fine. Along comes the skinny Medicine Flute, claiming he has had a vision placed over his eyes—a vision promising that your husband will instead sneak south to conspire with whites. And according to our own scouts, he is doing just that."

Sudden anger weakened Honey Eater's muscles. "You believe this?" she demanded.

"Niece, what *should* I believe when all appearances give the lie to his words? Yes, I despise this skinny bone blower. But tell me a thing. If he is always wrong, and your husband always right, why must I always take it on faith? You believe in

127

him. Fine. You are randy for his touch, and this is understandable in one as young as you. He is a fine buck to look on! But the singing in your blood, the heat he stirs in the depths of your womanhood, these have nothing to do with the truth of his words."

Honey Eater's anger had given way to cold dread. "Is this what the people are saying?" she demanded. "They believe Medicine Flute had a 'vision'? They do not see that all of this was the work of Wolf Who Hunts Smiling and Medicine Flute?"

Sharp Nosed Woman avoided her niece's eye this time. "No. They do not see it, and I do not see it. Of course these two wily Cheyennes are base plotters, few deny this. The issue is not their honesty, though few consider them so treacherous as your husband claims they are.

"No. Only, explain this, haughty one. How could Wolf Who Hunts Smiling possibly have controlled events so thoroughly that he could make Touch the Sky ride south, deserting his tribe without benefit of council or even explanation? It would need a shaman's power to do this. Are you saying Wolf Who Hunts Smiling is a shaman?"

But by now Honey Eater was too miserable to respond. She saw, clearly enough, how things stood in camp. Indeed, she was forced now to admit it to herself: She, too, suffered a raw, cankering nubbin of doubt. It was hard enough when Touch the Sky rode out to the mining camp. The people winked and grinned and shook their heads knowingly. For everyone knew by now that the white woman, Kristen Steele, lived there—the same woman Touch the Sky had often contrived to meet. However, Honey Eater had refused to let jealousy taint her love for Touch the Sky.

Now, again, she was forced to believe in Touch the Sky without knowing the reasons for her belief. Sharp Nosed Woman was right: Much about Touch the Sky must be taken on faith. But whose fault was that? With enemies constantly working to ruin him, how could he clear his name and prove his honor once and for all? Chased out of the white man's world, he was still being denied his rightful place in the red man's.

But justice was hardly the issue right now, she knew. Honey Eater watched as Touch the Sky's friend and supporter, Spotted Tail, crossed from his tipi to the Bow String soldier lodge. He walked openly, unconcerned. However, Honey Eater saw it as clearly as he did: Everywhere, the eyes of hostile Bull Whip troopers were also following Spotted Tail, leader of the Bow Strings. Although no one had said it, Honey Eater feared that Spotted Tail might soon be meeting with an 'accident.'

Logically, if not willingly, her glance shifted across the central clearing to Medicine Flute's tipi. As usual, it was surrounded by a throng of Bull Whip soldiers and other supporters. However, there was one conspicuous absence—Wolf Who Hunts Smiling. Alarm prickled at Honey Eater's scalp like invisible insects. Any time *that* one was gone, there was surely trouble in the wind.

Honey Eater trembled with disgust and fear when she recognized it: the flat, atonal notes of Medicine Flute's leg-bone instrument, mocking her. *Soon*, those hideous notes promised her. *Soon . . . and the worm will turn.*

* * *

Shortly after Sister Sun had risen from her birthplace in the east, Wolf Who Hunts Smiling spotted the signal he was searching for: two quick, black puffs of smoke rising above the southern horizon near Beaver Creek.

He smiled his wolf grin, lips curling back away from his teeth. Those signals were being sent by a Bull Whip stationed south of the Powder River Camp. It meant he had finally discovered it: a fresh track made by Touch the Sky's mare, heading north. Wolf Who Hunts Smiling had notched one of the pony's hooves for just this purpose.

He was standing on a long rise behind the Cheyenne camp. Below, mist still hung in pockets over the river and most in camp were still asleep. No one would even notice when he cut his pony out of the corral and rode out this early.

He knew the trail Touch the Sky was following to reach the Sans Arcs. And given the time pressures, the tall brave would have little luxury to be as vigilant as usual. He knew a perfect spot for ambushing him.

"This place hears me," Wolf Who Hunt Smiling said out loud, addressing the land and sky as far as he could see. "This time my enemy has no place to hide."

Touch the Sky forded Beaver Creek just before sunup, waging a harder battle against exhaustion than he did against the runoff-swollen creek.

He had left his parents' ranch soon after sunset the night before, even as the rest of the men turned to constructing the key defenses. Before he de-

130

parted, Touch the Sky conferred with his father. Then they buried that nitroglycerin gel in the one spot most vulnerable to sudden attack.

Two Twists, meantime, had insisted on riding as a vedette or mounted sentry, taking on the dangerous job of watching for an attack by Big Tree or his men while the defenders were exposed. Touch the Sky had no fear on the score of his friend's competence and fighting skill. But he had barely 18 seasons behind him—too green to be facing the fearsome Red Raider of the Plains.

This made two nights in a row now that Touch the Sky had substituted hard riding for sleep. He and his plucky little chestnut were feeling the strain. Still, Touch the Sky pushed his mount hard. He was like a man caught between the choice of sacrificing his wife or his babes. He could not be in two places at once, yet neither could he forego at least one more counsel with Caleb, Little Horse, and Tangle Hair. Not only were they up against Sis-ki-dee, but a Sis-ki-dee with the fire power of a bluecoat regiment.

The mare tried to slow from a run to a canter, but Touch the Sky tightened his knees hard, pushing her on. He bent low and spoke soothingly into her left ear.

"Fly, girl, and I promise you this. You'll rest up in the Sans Arcs with a full grain bag, and I'll borrow another horse for the ride back."

Either the words or his tone struck the chestnut as agreeable. She laid her ears back flat and surged forward.

Again Touch the Sky was tempted to lash himself to his pony and close his eyes for a few minutes. He knew she'd look after him, for they had become partners in the struggle for survival. But he fought down the temptation and kept his wary glance sweeping in a wide circle around him, scanning the rimrock and bluffs and coulees for signs of danger.

Wolf Who Hunts Smiling hobbled his pure black pony well back from the trail, leaving her in a patch of lush graze to insure her silence. He drew his Colt Model 1855 Rifle from its scabbard and untied the osage-wood bow from his rigging. Feet cushioned and silenced by two pair of elkskin moccasins, he took up an excellent position behind a huge granite boulder on a slope overlooking the trail.

Below, the trail took a sharp elbow bend that could not be avoided because of the steep slopes on either side. Even better, a bubbling freshet flowed just past the turn—the first sign of water after Beaver Creek, and the last to be had until one reached the Powder. No Indian who knew that trail ever passed without watering his pony there.

First, Wolf Who Hunts Smiling drew a handful of new, fire-hardened arrows from his quill and lay them and his bow down ready to hand. Next, he pulled a new paper cartridge from his war sash and tore it open with his teeth. He poured the powder down the barrel of his Colt percussion rifle and pushed the bullet in after with his thumb. He drew his ramrod and tamped the projectile down, then pulled back the hammer and placed a percussion cap on the nib.

He knew better than to lay his rifle along that

rock and sight in—as much as he hated White Man Runs Him, he was the first to praise his skill as a warrior. Give him the slightest warning, and a man might as well build his own scaffold.

Big Tree behind, Sis-ki-dee ahead, and Brother Ball waiting here to say hello. It made Wolf Who Hunts Smiling grin in spite of his genuine nervousness—and nervous he admitted he was, for no brave took lightly the killing of an enemy this worthy. Die he must, and soon, for surely no man ever had so many hard enemies sniffing his spoor.

But how fitting, he reminded himself, that this worthy one be felled by the same warrior whose coup feathers were stripped from his bonnet because of him.

Truly, Touch the Sky's hair was worth more than all coups ever counted. And if—

Wolf Who Hunts Smiling's thoughts scattered like flies when he felt slight vibrations in the boulder, then in the ground beneath him. A rider approaching.

Wolf Who Hunts Smiling stared at his cocked hammer and repeated the Cheyenne battle slogan adopted from their Sioux cousins: "One bullet, one enemy!"

"Slow down, girl," Touch the Sky urged his mare. "You'll get a bellyache."

The brave had flopped on his face to dip his head into the freshet. Man and horse drank greedily, Touch the Sky grateful for the ice-cold slap to his senses.

He lay there a long moment, senses alert but muscles relaxed, his head immersed in the cold mountain runoff. Then he sat back up, rivulets of cold water trickling from his long, unbraided locks. He watched the graceful curve of his pony's neck as she drank. It was a stolen moment of peace, and he took it without guilt.

He scanned the high ground around him as he rose, tired joints protesting. Normally, if he were not so exhausted, he might profitably consult with his 'shaman sense' in the search for danger. But when his other senses were as strained as they were now, Touch the Sky worried he might confuse premonition with the frazzled nerves of fatigue.

It seemed quiet enough, though. He decided to take a chance and let his pony drink a little longer—she was reluctant to pull her head back when he tugged on her hackamore.

Lost in thought, he barely paid attention to the slight prickling high on his chest. A red ant, perhaps, picked up when he lay in the grass to drink. He swiped vaguely at his chest.

The prickle became an uncomfortable pinch. Now Touch the Sky glanced down—and felt the blood drain from his face.

Even as he watched, the lone grizzly claw on his leather thong broke the surface of his skin and drew blood!

The shock of it forced English from Touch the Sky's lips: "God have mercy on my soul!" But the Indian in him took over a heartbeat later, understanding this warning from Arrow Keeper.

Instinct made him combine the two actions into one movement. The closest object to hand was the obsidian knife in its beaded sheath on his sash.

Making sure the blade didn't strike her, Touch the Sky threw the knife, handle first, hard toward his pony and shouted "Hi-ya, *hii*-ya!" even as he tucked and rolled hard, splashing unceremoniously into the water.

The bone handle struck the pony's withers. The startled, well-trained mustang leaped forward across the freshet and raced to cover, a battle pattern taught to all Cheyenne ponies.

Touch the Sky heard the bullet thwack into the grass behind him a split second before he heard the rifle discharge. Then he was racing to catch up with his pony, arrows fanning him so closely, that the fletching burned traces in his skin.

Chapter Thirteen

Leery of meeting in an enclosed place with an enemy so near, the three Cheyennes hunkered down to counsel in the midst of the saddle-band stock in the rope corral at the center of camp.

"Caleb Riley was shot," Little Horse said bluntly, "and close enough to his lights to kill a lesser man. Yet, brother, I swear by the earth I live on, he came up roaring the he-bear talk and fanning his Colt."

"He missed them," Tangle Hair put in excitedly, "but brother, you should have seen Caleb! The war face he gave them sent green dung down their ponies' legs! A hole in his chest big enough to cache venison, and that pale warrior roaring like a bull! It left fire in us, brother! I never took this blond beard for a squaw man, for I know his brother Tom. But this thing he did, it came from a fire within. I will sing it at my clan lodge."

Touch the Sky raised one hand, silencing his friends. Despite the troubles heaping up on him like an avalanche, Touch the Sky could not help smiling. This was typical of Indian braves, not only boasting of their own feats after combat, but making a point to sing the deeds of other brave men, for bravery is the hardest thing and must always be told.

"Bucks, Caleb Riley is straight grain clear through. I will speak with him soon enough and thank him for his courage. Just as I thank both of you now for your own. Indeed, in remaining loyal to me, you have been forced to courage as a daily virtue."

His friends could not miss a certain bitterness in Touch the Sky's tone—nor blame him for it.

"Better that," Little Horse said, "than the base, cowardly treachery of those who have forced us to it. *Us*, tall warrior, not you alone."

"Yes," Tangle Hair said. "So our lives are dangerous since crossing our lances over yours? So. Our lives are dangerous. I agree with this sturdy horse who just spoke. Buck, Big Tree tried to kill your mother! Sis-ki-dee meant to bull the women, then stake them down for all his men to top. And such as these are the 'men' our own Wolf Who Hunts Smiling has unleashed on you. He himself just tried to kill you. Do not succumb to pity and turn your rage inward—you have been far more wronged than wrong."

"From this instant on," Little Horse threw in, "let your thoughts be bloody or nothing else. I am with you until the Last Battle, Bear Caller."

Nothing could have rallied Touch the Sky's resolve more than this eloquent show of loyalty from two warriors second to none. But it was not the Indian way to dwell on things close to the heart. Immediately, the talk turned practical.

"Brother," Touch the Sky said to Little Horse, "you are sure the ponies gained strength after you touched the claw?"

"Believe it, buck. You spoke straight. Arrow Keeper is in those claws."

"I have believed it right along, Little Horse. Now you must believe it. I am leaving my pony here to rest and taking a fast horse from among these. Soon comes the attack, both down south and right here. And count upon it, they will be timed so that I can choose only one."

"As you say," Tangle Hair said. "And we would think less of you if you did not choose to be down south. But it would truly comfort me if you were with us for this fight, brother."

"Then be comforted, for I will be."

"But you just said—"

Tangle Hair fell silent when Touch the Sky dipped one hand into his parfleche. He handed an object to Little Horse.

"Do you recognize it?"

Curiosity evident in his face, Little Horse examined the whistle made from highly polished bone decorated with dyed feathers. Finally he nodded.

"It is a war whistle," he said. "The Lakota sometimes use them. They blow them during an important battle. It is said they make the cry of the eagle, which calls the thunder to the warrior's aid."

It was Touch the Sky's turn to nod. "It was Arrow Keeper's. He told me once that it must be used only when the moment is right. Blow it too soon or too late, there is no medicine. Keep it, Little Horse. And use it as Arrow Keeper said."

Little Horse looked doubtful. "Brother, how can *I* know such a thing? I am not trained for a shaman."

"Maiyun is not limited, buck, only to shamen. He may choose to work medicine through any of His children. Know this. Though we will be far apart, we will work this medicine together. Attend to the claw around your neck, watch for the sign. When it comes, sound that whistle with all your heart, and look for the thunder."

"Thunder?" Tangle Hair echoed, his eyes wide with awe as he examined this beautiful whistle, so much finer than Medicine Flute's crude bone instrument. "What manner of thunder, brother?"

But it was Little Horse who spoke. "No questions, Tangle Hair. No more discussion of things holy. Faith alone makes them real."

With that, Little Horse slid the war whistle into his legging sash. Despite his limitless courage, Little Horse was a practical man who preferred to follow others in matters not relating to battle. So of course his eyes showed the deep doubts he still felt. However, his voice was calm and sure when he added:

"With the help of the High Holy Ones and our shaman here, I will do what must be done or die in the attempt."

* * *

"The stakes are portable," Corey explained, pride tinging his voice. "I made 'em light but sturdy, we can set them puppies anywhere we want."

"Bark's still on most the wood," Knobby added. "Goldang rough to see at night. Catch 'em-air hosses right in their vitals."

"We'll spread them out on the best approach slopes after dark," John Hanchon said. "I burned wide firebreaks today. They can't burn us out by setting the outlying hay stubble ablaze. The buildings're still vulnerable to fire arrows, though."

Touch the Sky nodded, though secretly he shared a knowing glance with young Two Twists. To them, the defenses seemed puny indeed in the face of Big Tree's inventive treachery. Indeed, even now as the men inspected the defenses, they kept a wary eye out and avoided standing in one spot too long.

"They hit while I was gone?" he asked.

John nodded, his big, bluff face tightening. "No hands hurt, thank God. But they throat-slashed all my beef cattle down at the mouth of Thompson's Canyon. Two Twists here found them."

Two Twists did not recognize his name when It was spoken, for Touch the Sky had given only the English translation to these white men. Indians believed their names lost power if spoken by hair faces.

"Them gut-eatin' bastards di'n' eat a one of 'em," Evan Blackford said. The foreman's voice was tight with anger and disgust. "Instead, they're eatin' horses. Study on it."

"Nothin' to study," Knobby assured him. "Comanch likes the taste of horse meat, 'n' so does the Apache. Both tribes'll eat mule before they'll eat beef, 'n' horse meat before any of 'em. Evan Blackford, you're a damn good foreman and they're ain't no yellow bone in ye. But doan go lookin' fir your own grave by gettin' all lathered agin the Injin. Stay frosty, shoot plumb, doan let 'em get you all wrathy, son. That's what they're aimin' to do—get you so bone-crushin' mad you can't rightly think straight. Then you're a gone coon."

Evan dismissed the old man with a careless wave. "Old dogs should stay on the porch."

Knobby cocked his head. He made no threatening gesture with the old Kentucky over-and-under tucked into the crook of his arm. But its side-mounted "mule ear" hammers and mile-long barrel made it hard to ignore.

"My gal Patsy Plumb here is an old dog, too," he said calmly. "But that ol' gal kin take your oysters off at a hunnert paces."

"You two lower your hammers," John said. "Knobby's right about one thing. Sarah's better now, sitting up and eating with a good appetite, thank God. But something she just told me sounded like Knobby talking.

"She said these Indians need killing, all right. But not because they're Indians. Because they're criminal trash, the same as the plug-uglies and Know Nothings terrorizing our cities back in the States."

By now the group of men had circled back around to the house.

"Why the shallow trench?" Touch the Sky said, pointing to a hastily dug trench—hardly deeper than a swale or a wallow—dug near the front of the house.

"Nuther one of my brilliant inventions," Corey boasted.

"Look yonder," Knobby said without pointing, not wanting to call attention if Comanches were watching them. "Corner of the house."

Touch the Sky spotted a hogshead within touching distance of one of the shuttered and loop-holed front windows.

"Coal oil," Corey said. "Won't burn in the barrel if they shoot an arrow into it. But it will if it's spread open to air. See that wooden trough? The hogshead sits on an angle and can be tipped from the house, the coal oil flooded into the trench. Toss fire on it, we'll have one hell of a flaming moat. All horses hate fire."

"Some of the hands dug rifle pits between here and the bunkhouse, case we get waylaid outside," John explained. "And we've dug hundreds of post holes, especially on that vulnerable slope behind the house. They have good horses, I know. But these holes'll give them Sam Hill. Everybody's been warned to stay clear of that spot where we planted your nitro pack."

Yes, Touch the Sky thought, Big Tree was fearsome. None more so, unless it be Sis-ki-dee or Wolf Who Hunts Smiling. And yet, his father and his friends had done well here. These defenses *were* good. They would not be enough, surely. It would take blood, no doubt human lives. It would take courage and fighting spirit and superb fighting skills. But these defenses just might prove the difference between a noble last stand and a possible victory.

Arrow Keeper was right: *The white man's cunning. . . .*

But cunning would not be enough, Arrow Keeper had warned. For a moment, Touch the Sky's fingers rose and made light contact with the grizzly claw around his neck.

Tangle Hair rode in to the heart of the Far West Mining Company's camp just before sunset. His face remained impassive as he led his pony toward the common corral. Caleb was still confined to his bed. But Liam and Little Horse, their faces anxious, were waiting there for his report. And both men saw instantly that Tangle Hair's face had lost some of its copper color.

The big Irish gang boss had picked up a smattering of Cheyenne and Sioux words and was adept at the universal hand signals used by Plains Indians. When he missed a word or two, Tangle Hair signed.

"Sis-ki-dee's men are massing for some kind of charge," the brave reported. "Or more likely, some kind of strike. They look confident, even sporting. I could not get so close as I wanted. But they have some kind of weapons there"—he pointed high up on the slopes around them—"and there."

"Them goddamn Requa batteries," Liam muttered in English, forgetting who his listeners were in his preoccupation. "Got to be. And not thing one we can do without gettin' our asses shot off. That's high ground. Plus, they got more grenades and nitro."

His meaning was so clear in his tone that the two Cheyennes needed no translator. Liam had just fallen silent when all the men heard it again: mocking laughter and catcalls, emanating from the ridges around them. Sis-ki-dee's brand of nerve warfare. It had been going on for days now, interspersed with the occasional grenade blast or sniping incident.

It wouldn't take much more of this, Little Horse knew, before some of the miners were driven to the brink of madness. Again the worried young Cheyenne warrior wondered: *Could* he do what Touch the Sky expected of him? Always, for every major battle such as this one, Touch the Sky had been there, somehow rallying the rest of them even when things seemed most forlorn and hopeless.

Little Horse would face any foe he could see, even if it meant sure death. But Touch the Sky needed him to help work medicine, to help in the world of things unseen. Could he?

Liam left to make his report to Caleb. Little Horse became aware that Tangle Hair was watching him. Tangle Hair, too, was frightened. Little Horse saw it in the vague focus of his eyes, the way he constantly scanned the ridges surrounding them.

"Tangle Hair?"

He looked at Little Horse. "I have ears, buck."

"Good. Do you know what Touch the Sky told me when we faced sure death on Wes Munro's keelboat? 'Little Horse,' he said, as if all his life he had waited for that moment, 'we have played our part well through the farce of life. *Now* we will

144

show them how a Cheyenne can die!' "

Tangle Hair grinned, then nodded. *"Ipewa,"* he said. "Good."

But again, from the ridges above them, more catcalls and shouted obscenities. Little Horse glanced again toward the ridges, and then beyond to the shrouded peak of Wendigo Mountain. It was Arrow Keeper who had taken him aside, many, many seasons ago, and pointed out that mountain. And when he did, the old shaman said simply: *The worst trouble in the world is there.*

And now, thought Little Horse, that trouble is here.

Chapter Fourteen

The new dawn was still a pale, insubstantial promise over the eastern horizon when Touch the Sky,
his fingertips lightly feeling the ground in front of
the house, said, "Here they come."

"Close?" John Hanchon said.

Touch the Sky stood up. "Vibrations are still
faint. They're sweeping down on us from those ra-
zor backs north of the valley. Unless it's a feint,
which it could be, this attack will be at the front
of the house."

"Jesus, we need to know which way!" Evan
Blackford complained, his voice tight with nervousness. Both Touch the Sky and Old Knobby
watched him closely. The man was not frightened,
which bothered them, as experienced warriors
knew that a sane fighter always felt fear. Rather,
he was agitated, made "blood simple" by the pros-

pect of revenge against these heathens.

"No need to get your pennies in a bunch," Knobby said. "Ain't nobody short of the Celestial Gent Himself has got a window on the Comanche's thinkin'."

"My guess is, it's no feint this time," Touch the Sky said. "Big Tree is no fool who does the obvious thing. He knows that back slope is an easier approach, so he's likely to figure we've concentrated our defenses there."

"Then let's play it that way," John decided. "We can't stand around with our thumbs up our sitters, playing guessing games. I'd rather make a choice—half a chance is better than none."

"Speak the truth and shame the devil, John Hanchon!" Knobby grinned. "I'm startin' to kallate how it ain't jist Injin ways what made Matthew here tough as leather. He's a red son now, mebbe, but he's got you and Sarah writ all over him."

Corey and Evan ran forward to position the pointed stakes along the northern approach. John Hanchon went out to share this latest news with the wranglers in the bunkhouse, who immediately took up positions in the newly dug rifle pits. They were placed to offer the best possible protection for both the house and the mustangs bunched in the corrals.

Soon no one had to place fingertips on the ground to detect the attack. The murmuring rhythm of hoofbeats gradually increased in volume, though it was still far too dark to discern any movement.

John returned, followed by Corey and Evan, all three men grim-faced as the fight now became a

Judd Cole

looming reality. They immediately took a bucket of powder and balls up through the ceiling trap in the attic, out onto the roof of the house. It was Old Knobby's job to stay downstairs with Sarah and hold the first floor by firing through the loopholed walls.

As for the Cheyennes, true to their blood they would not fort up for this fight. They knew they could inflict more damage fighting from horseback. Thus, they had the critical job of roving attackers, relying on the Cheyenne's superb skirmishing skills to break the attack before it reached the house.

The mutter of hooves had become a rolling thunder. Touch the Sky made a final check of the house, making sure Sarah was secure in an interior room with no windows. She had not flinched when John laid the Colt revolver on the counterpane covering her. Then the two Cheyennes went outside and swung up onto their battle-rigged mounts.

Though Touch the Sky missed his chestnut, he had wisely selected a Sioux-trained mustang from Caleb's saddle band. The little calico would be dependable and quick, and no Indian could hope to outride Comanches, anyway.

"Ride into that copse over there," Touch the Sky told Two Twists, pointing to a spot east of the yard. "I will take up a position between those haystacks to the west. We must weaken their flanks, little brother, so those in the lodge can concentrate on the main body. It is usually the flankers who ride in for the kill."

"I may die," Two Twists said with an exagger-

148

ated swagger. "What of that? *Watch* me free a Comanche soul before I cross over!"

"You may live, too, fool, and thus enjoy killing more of them some day. I did not bring you down here to die, stout brave! Fighters like you are as rare as the white buffalo. Kill our enemy, yes. But also live to fight another day. Hi-ya, hii-*ya*!"

"Hi-ya! Hii-*ya*!"

The two warriors crossed lances, then whirled their ponies and flew to their battle stations. Only moments later, a hideous death cry separated itself from the approaching din—the death cry of a pony impaling itself on pointed stakes, the cry even more terrifying than a man's. Another horse whinnied fiercely as it jabbed a foreleg into a post hole, snapping the bone like a green stick.

But though the attack was slowed, it was not broken. Now yipping Comanche braves began to stream past the last stakes, still insubstantial targets in the grainy half-light of dawn. Muzzles spat fire as wranglers in the rifle pits fired into the din, hoping to score a hit.

All they managed, however, was to waste their ammunition and give away their positions. Unable to see what was happening, Touch the Sky and Two Twists nonetheless heard it with grisly clarity: a wrangler, surrounded by Comanches, piteously calling for help. His cry ended in a banshee shriek of terror and pain. By now a coop was burning, and in the flickering light Touch the Sky saw a Comanche brave holding high his lance, bloody genitals impaled on the tip.

It was going badly, worse than Touch the Sky expected. He saw Two Twists boldly ride forward, launching arrow after arrow. Then, quicker than a blink, his pony caught a fatal slug and crashed to the ground hard, flinging the Cheyenne and snapping his leg at an impossible angle.

Touch the Sky emptied his Sharps, then dropped it into its scabbard and switched to arrows. But his position had been spotted, and now the Comanche attackers rained their own flint-tipped arrows in on him.

At first, the unexpected resistance from the house surprised the attackers and caused them to fade back. Old Knobby's over-and-under roared with double charges of black powder, the three marksmen on the roof kept up a nonstop hail of lead.

Touch the Sky saw Evan Blackford, his face wild with battle frenzy, rise up from the roof and drop a Comanche pony with his Volcanic lever-action repeater. His next shot dropped the fleeing brave.

"That was for Dez Gillycuddy's widow, you red vermin!" he screamed down at the Indians.

"Cover down, you jackass!" Touch the Sky heard Corey roar.

"Cover down, my sweet aunt!" Evan shouted back. "We *got* the sonsabitches now!"

It was then that Touch the Sky, forced to cover down or die, watched Big Tree separate himself from the attackers and rush the house. Evan fired, fired again, continuously cocking the lever, until Big Tree launched a throwing tomahawk that sliced clean through Evan's breastbone, opening him up like butcher's meat. He flew from the roof in a spray of blood, a death cry on his lips.

Big Tree's bloody handiwork rallied his braves. Now they were grouping for a final assault on the house.

Touch the Sky barely managed to break cover, gallop to the fallen Two Twists, and drag the injured brave to safety under a buckboard. But the intensity of the Comanche arrows made it impossible to rush them by himself.

It's up to Pa and Corey now, he told himself. Then came John's desperate shout. "Knobby! You hear me down there? My firing pin broke! Fire up that trench, or they'll overrun us!"

Big Tree, yipping fiercely, dropped his lance and the charge was on. The rest happened with nightmare rapidity. Touch the Sky saw one of the shuttered windows bang open, saw Old Knobby's arms snake out, tilting the hogshead filled with coal oil. Its contents gushed down the wooden chute Corey made and filled the shallow trench out front. Old Knobby's arm snaked out one more time, and a flaming torch arced through the air.

But in his hurry, the old man made a crucial miscalculation: he tossed the torch over the shallow, oil-filled trench. It landed one foot beyond it and lay there flickering uselessly!

"Can you shoot, Two Twists?"

"I think so, but—"

"One bullet, one enemy, buck! Cover me!"

Touch the Sky leaped his Sioux-trained mustang, dug into her flanks hard with his heels, and slid forward into the classic defensive riding position invented by Cheyennes: He gripped the pony around her neck and covered his body with hers, leaving only his head visible down below her

151

chest as he watched his enemies. Not only did he thus reduce the target he offered the Comanches, but he would also be ready when the moment came to save that house and everyone in it.

At first, intent on the charge, Big Tree and his warriors thought the mustang was riderless, one who leaped the corral and was now made giddy from panic. Touch the Sky approached hard from the west, his enemies from the north. He was rapidly bearing down on the front of the house when Big Tree and a brave in a bone breastplate realized what was happening.

The Comanche in the breastplate shifted his stolen Army carbine for an easy shot at Touch the Sky's pony. Then, behind him, Touch the Sky heard Two Twist's bow fwip, and an arrow punched into the brave's left eye, exiting clean from the back of his skull and dropping him from his saddle like a sack of grain.

Big Tree, always keen for a challenge and a chance to show off, disdained killing the horse. He saved his prowess for Touch the Sky, launching arrow after arrow seemingly without even stringing them. They fanned by his head, so close they droned like blow flies. But he could not duck back, for now he approached the trench and the still-burning—though only faintly—torch.

Taking an incredible risk, but forced to it, Touch the Sky leaned even further down. The mustang's flank heaved beneath him, threatening to toss him with every step. Then, swift as thought, the torch was there and he swatted hard and knocked it into the trench.

But it went out! he told himself with sick despair. *I was too late, it—*

KA-WHUMPH!

The trench went up with a sound like a giant gas pocket igniting. The force of it panicked his mustang and made her instantly crow-hop. But it had a like effect on the Comanche horses.

A wall of flame curled up, followed by a huge, belching puff of thick black smoke. One pony stopped so hard that her rider flew over his hackamore and into the burning oil. The shrieks he raised, as he was quickly boiled in oil, unnerved his comrades as surely as the flames unnerved their ponies. Those who could control their mounts whirled them about and broke back toward the outlying ridges. Those who could not deserted their horses and bolted on foot—which proved, Touch the Sky thought, how frightened these Comanches were. For they were loathe to be separated from their ponies in combat.

Corey kept lead nipping at their heels, Old Knobby's big stovepipe rifle assisting the defense. As Big Tree, seeing which way the wind set for now, whirled to join his fleeing men, his eyes met Touch the Sky's.

"Well done, Bear Caller!" he called out, clearly enjoying this sport. "The Noble Red Man triumphs yet again. But one cut does not bleed Big Tree to death! Your mother is not alive right now because I failed to kill her. I only wounded her because I plan to top her, in front of your eyes, before I kill her! Your clever white man's tricks have been exhausted. The next charge breaks you, I swear it!"

153

Chapter Fifteen

Since being hired to teach school at the mining camp, Kristen Steele had her own small but serviceable dwelling beside the schoolhouse, a one-room cabin with a puncheon floor and small sleeping loft. But after the recent kidnap attempt, and Caleb's injury, she had moved in with the Rileys temporarily to assist her friend Woman Dress.

Caleb had devised a last-minute plan for evacuating the women and children by a special hired train. But the resourceful Blackfoot warriors had destroyed a long stretch of track about halfway between the mining camp and Register Cliffs. Until that track could be repaired, they were all trapped here in this hollow. As vulnerable as a bird's nest on the ground, as Liam McKinney had aptly put it.

Kristen knew she had no place to run, anyway.

Somewhere out there on the Plains roamed her father, looking to kill Matthew—and now, since she had fled his tyranny, her too. All these thoughts and more were roiling in her troubled mind when the Requa artillery rifles opened up on the ridges above them.

She sat bolt upright on the horsehair mattress, a scream caught in her throat. The noise, shattering the peace of the morning's pre-dawn stillness, was totally unnerving. Each time one of the batteries fired its 25 barrels, it sounded like a huge ice flow cracking apart. The reverberating echo smashed through the camp like some vindictive storm, almost as terrible as the bullets now raining down on them.

"Don't move, Kristen!" Caleb hollered from the bedroom. "Keep away from doors and windows and *don't* run outside!"

But even as he fell silent, slugs punched through the mud-chinked walls and made both Kristen and Woman Dress scream in terror. The Indians had maliciously concentrated their aim on the housing area. Piteous cries went up as occupants were struck through their walls. Others, foolishly panicking, ran out into the streets to be cut down like saplings in a hailstorm.

A reverberating explosion shook the floor under Kristen's mattress; then another, and another, so close they rattled the dishes in the kitchen and shook the Currier and Ives lithographs off the walls.

"They're flipping grenades down on us!" Caleb shouted. "Christ on a broomtail, they're goin' the whole hog! This is a helluva time for me to be stove up in bed! Listen, you two! Hear it? Our boys are fighting back! Calm down and don't—"

More rounds chunked through the walls as the Requa batteries spit death and destruction down on them. Another grenade exploded, this one so close it shattered the window glass Caleb had hand-carried from the trading post at Red Shale. Kristen screamed and buried her face in the blankets as shards of deadly glass and debris blasted the room.

Tangle Hair was snatching a few minutes badly needed rest, and Little Horse was riding sentry throughout the camp, when the Requas opened up.

Little Horse froze for several heartbeats, the noise so fierce it seemed to unhinge his muscles from his will. Wherever the concentrated rounds struck, they had the effect of a giant fist, smashing anything that got in front of them. Entire walls collapsed, stacks of wood went flying, horses bunched tight for protection only to die as one when sheets of lead swept them.

By the time Little Horse made it back to Tangle Hair, the grenades, too, were adding to the terror and confusion.

"Brother, we have no targets!" Tangle Hair shouted in wild-eyed frustration. Grenade flashes illuminated the two desperate braves in stark glimpses. Tangle Hair pointed up toward the rim-rock. "Now we see the muzzle flashes clearly, but they keep moving the guns."

Little Horse nodded grimly. All around them panicked stock whickered and brayed, adding to the din of male shouts and female screams. A group of about a half-dozen miners were advancing behind Liam McKinney toward the west end of camp, hoping to position themselves to stymie the final charge when it came.

"They are clustered too tight," Little Horse said. "They must fan out!"

But he had no English to shout a warning. The next moment his face went pale in horror as the group caught a Requa blast flush, scattering them just as white men at the trading post loved to scatter their ninepins. Those men who weren't killed outright lay screaming, one begging someone to shoot him and finish the job the "covered-bridge gun" had started.

"Brother!" Tangle Hair shouted, so agitated he no longer held his face impassive as warriors did. "This is a slaughter! Is this the time Touch the Sky spoke of? The time to blow the war whistle and summon the thunder to our aid?"

But Little Horse only shook his head, miserable. Touch the Sky had said he would know when the time had come. Had the sign come, and had he missed it? If he blew that whistle too soon, Touch the Sky had warned him, the medicine would be destroyed.

But how much longer could he hold off? *Faith*, Touch the Sky had assured him. No matter how grim events turned, he must never lose faith. Once that was gone, spirit power was useless.

"Touch the Sky will not let us down" Little Horse assured his worried companion, hoping against hope that his words were true.

*   *   *

157

Despite his proud boast, Big Tree had no plans for a final, bloody assault if it could be avoided. Touch the Sky was not surprised when the Comanches first set the grass on fire, trying to burn the whites out.

But John Hanchon's firebreaks held. While the Comanches were thus occupied, the defenders steeled themselves for the final assault. John went down into the yard and retrieved the dead Evan's Volcanic rifle. Then he checked on the wranglers and went to make one last inspection of the firebreaks.

With Two Twists wounded, and Evan and several other hands killed, Sarah insisted on joining the fight. She stationed herself in the critical spot between Old Knobby and the ladder leading to the roof, a bucket of balls and powder at her feet. Two Twists had not liked the idea of being taken into the house. But since Touch the Sky gave the order, he obediently took up a spot in front of a loophole: As fast as Sarah could charge the rifles, he intended to free Comanche souls.

As for Touch the Sky: Despite being up against superior horsemen on an unfamiliar pony, he had no intention of giving up his roving-warrior duty outside. Everyone else was trapped inside this house. One of them had to be outside to seize any opportunity that presented itself. Every instinct as a red warrior told him so.

"That's it," John reported, coming in from the east flank, his face smeared with soot. "The firebreaks held, they're giving up on that idea. I saw them massing out past the winter pastures. The trench out front is burned out. They're getting set to attack."

"Never mind that trench," Touch the Sky said. "I don't think they'll try to bridge the gap from the front this time. They'll feint that way, but they won't be eager to eat so much lead now. Pa, you and Corey watch behind the house, too. Knobby, be ready—if they disappear suddenly, get your keester to the back of the house." Touch the Sky nodded at Sarah. "And make sure she stays covered down."

"She don't," Knobby promised, "I'll sap 'er upside the skull pan and make *sure* she covers down."

Touch the Sky translated the necessary points quickly for Two Twists, then hurried back outside to his mount. The tall brave grabbed handfuls of mane and was about to swing up when he felt it: that familiar pinching in his chest.

He reached down to touch the bear claw around his neck. One finger came away with a few drops of blood on it.

"Now," he said out loud, his heart racing, "Little Horse and the rest are up against it!" He gripped the claw tightly for a long moment, willing a strong image of Little Horse on the screen of his mind.

"Now, brother," he murmured. "*Now* you must wake to the spirit world or your living world is doomed!"

"Now comes the sun, brother," Tangle Hair said, despair clear in his voice. "See up there, past the lodgepole timber? The majority of Sis-ki-dee's braves, massed for the finishing attack. With the coming of daylight, they can advance under cover of the Requa guns. We cannot even take up decent positions against them, they mow us down."

"Here they come!" a miner bellowed. "Move up to protect the houses!"

Little Horse didn't understand the English words, but he recognized the hopeless yet determined desperation of the tone well enough. He had just recharged his revolving-barrel shotgun when a sharp pain made him glance down.

A drop of blood zigzagged down his chest.

Tangle Hair stared, hope flaring in his eyes, when Little Horse seized the decorated war whistle from his parfleche and brought it to his lips.

Oddly, the Requa guns and grenades and rifles suddenly fell silent as the frightened brave blew hard into the whistle. The lone, high-pitched, crystal clear note emanating from it seemed to swell far beyond its original sound as it rose up from the hollow, washing over the trees and ridges and caves and cutbanks surrounding them.

At first there was nothing. The long silence drew out until one of Sis-ki-dee's men fired another burst from a Requa battery.

A moment later, however, the 'thunder' did indeed come to the defenders' aid.

The huge, collective roar was so ferocious that, at first, Little Horse wondered if they weren't better off with the artillery guns blasting on them. It was the kill cry of the fearsome grizzly—repeated over and over as every silvertip bear in the area converged on those Blackfoot braves up on the ridges.

At first the attackers were frozen, incredulous. Then, as they realized the silvertips were indeed attacking, somebody yelled out, "The Bear Caller must be back! We are doomed!"

Panic ensued. At that same moment, a huge, shaggy yellow she-grizz burst into view behind one of the Requa batteries. She picked it—and the screaming Blackfoot firing it—up and hurled them out off the high ridge.

Below, cheers erupted from the miners as the bears continued to rout the Blackfoot attackers.

"Brother, look!"

Tangle Hair pointed off to the left above them. Sis-ki-dee and his lackey Scalp Cane were fleeing down a faint game trace when a huge grizzly reared up in front of them, curved claws fanning the air. While the Cheyennes watched, Sis-ki-dee whirled his agile pony and fled.

Scalp Cane, however, hurled one of the Adam's hand grenades at the bear. But in his nervous haste, he botched the movement when he jerked the wrist strap to remove the pin. The grenade hitched in midair, then bounced down at Scalp Cane's feet. Turning white, he bent to pick it up and throw it again. His face was about a foot above the grenade when it detonated, leaving human paste on the rocks all around.

Despite the death and destruction all around them, the two Cheyennes could not help falling on the ground in helpless laughter at Scalp Cane's foolish death. But even as he shook with welcome mirth, Little Horse worried about Touch the Sky down south, facing the superb Comanche warriors under Big Tree. Nor could Little Horse forget what he had just witnessed: Sis-ki-dee, once again escaping to loose his murderous treachery on the world.

Chapter Sixteen

"That was Jeb Flemming they castrated," Corey called out grimly from the rooftop, where the view was none too pretty. "And he took an arrow in his legs a few days ago! God-in-whirlwinds! He pulled his own freight and then some."

"Never even collected his fightin' wages," Knobby answered from behind his loopholed shutter downstairs. John's hands earned forty dollars a month, but range custom held that a man received extra pay for fighting rustlers and Indians.

"His ma's still alive and living in Laramie," John said. "She'll get it. That is, if. . . . "

John trailed off, cursing himself for a fool and hoping Sarah didn't hear him. He came damn near to saying *if we survive this*.

"I reckon there's some," Corey said, glancing

down toward his Cheyenne friend in the yard, "don't *ever* collect fightin' wages, though they spend plenty of time on the scrap."

"I can think of better ways to make a living," Touch the Sky called back, still staring north to monitor their enemy as they massed to charge.

"There's a home truth," Knobby said. "Was a time, I figured you fir a clerk in your pa's store. And here you are, totin' more battle scars than a Sioux war shield. Ain't life a case o' the drizzlin' shits, boy?"

"Knobby!" Touch the Sky heard his scandalized mother call out. "I realize you men are on the battlefield, and I'm proud of all of you. But I'll have you remember there's a lady present! You watch your mouth!"

"Drat my bones!" Knobby said, genuinely contrite. "This hoss is pure-dee sorry, Sarah Hanchon."

"Here they come!" Touch the Sky shouted. "Remember, be set to defend either the front or the back of the house. Chances are good they'll use a smaller force to divert the front while the main body swings around behind.

"Whatever you do, don't offer a line of fire to that big, ugly red bastard riding the ginger. That's Big Tree. He's the one you want to try concentrating your fire on. Two Twists!" Touch the Sky added, switching suddenly to Cheyenne.

"I have ears, shaman!"

"Yes, and a clout, too. Make sure you leave it on this time. My mother is in there."

Both braves surprised the rest by laughing at this private exchange—a reference to the bold

Two Twists's habit of lifting his clout at his enemies in battle to taunt them.

But the joking was over, and the fight was coming to them. Touch the Sky made one last visual check, then swung his pony around to the side of the house and took up a position behind one corner of the "four-holer," as Corey proudly called the new outhouse he'd recently built.

By now Touch the Sky and his Sioux-broken mount had gained valuable knowledge about each other's battle styles and abilities. More confident than he had been during the first Comanche charge, the Cheyenne was determined to be more effective this time at harassing and diverting the enemy—his main goal, of course, being to kill Big Tree. But that had often proved an elusive goal, and he had no plans to sacrifice his family and friends to the thirst for revenge.

He checked the load in his Sharps, the tension of his buffalo-sinew bowstring, made sure his stone-tipped lance and his steel-bladed throwing axe were ready to hand in the pony's battle rigging. Then, as the wranglers opened up from their rifle pits, Touch the Sky loosed a war whoop and heeled his pony hard.

Big Tree was well out ahead, out of range. But Touch the Sky caught the right flank completely by surprise. Immediately assuming the offensive, he drew a bead on the first brave to come under his sights. Touch the Sky's Sharps bucked in his hands, the brave flew from his pony, and the Cheyenne immediately tossed his empty rifle aside.

Now several Comanches had spotted him. Touch the Sky seized his throwing axe and tossed it hard in one fluid movement. It spun end-over-end, then neatly cleft the skull of a charging Comanche. Never once hesitating, for hesitation meant death, he tugged his hair bridle hard to make his pony veer. Simultaneously, he gripped his lance and sent it into the belly of a third warrior, not killing him but taking him out of the fight.

In the space of a few eyeblinks, three Comanches were thus dead or down. Now Touch the Sky seized a handful of arrows from his foxskin quiver, still desperately searching for Big Tree. The defenders in the house were throwing up a stiff wall of lead, managing to shoot several of the attackers' ponies out from under them.

At this moment Touch the Sky was almost indistinguishable from his Comanche foes. He bounced atop his pony, holding on only with his legs as he launched arrow after arrow into the swirling midst of his enemy. But more and more Comanches were training their fire on him. The agile Sioux pony saved his life time and again, constantly swerving and therefore giving the Comanches precious little at which to aim.

Then, in a heartbeat, things went all to hell.

From the corner of one eye, Touch the Sky saw Corey drop his rifle as blood blossomed from his chest. Then Sarah screamed from downstairs, the sound turning Touch the Sky's blood to ice.

"Knobby!" she shouted, even as the return fire from within slowed when the old trapper was hit.

A moment later a bullet found his pony's lights, and Touch the Sky was down. No pony, his father and Two Twists the only riflemen still defending the house. And the wounded Two Twists could not move quickly to the back of the house—a critical detail, for now Big Tree led his yipping cohort quickly around to the back of the house, just as Touch the Sky had predicted.

John Hanchon, warned by his adopted son beforehand, was ready. His steady aim forced them to fade back for a charge. Desperate, knowing this rush would be the end of the beleaguered defenders, Touch the Sky glanced up the long slope. His eyes found a small spot where the ground had been newly dug up.

That nitro gel was buried there, close to the surface and protected only by a thin layer of dirt. Since nitroglycerin was highly susceptible to concussive blows, he and his father hoped a direct hit by a charging pony's hoof might detonate it.

But the Comanches had massed much farther over and had already begun their charge. To make matters worse, the back door slapped open and Sarah stepped outside, aiming Knobby's old Kentucky rifle! The determined look on her face announced that she was prepared to die fighting alongside her husband and son.

So shaken he cursed in English, Touch the Sky drew his knife and ran out into plain view of the attacking Indians.

The sight must have looked ridiculous to Big Tree and his men: This lone Cheyenne on foot facing at least a dozen mounted warriors—and nothing in his hand but a knife! Either it was suicidal or rabbit-brained. Whichever, the temptation was too great to pass up. Big Tree slapped his pony's neck on the right side with the reins, and the entire charge swerved directly toward Touch the Sky.

Again Touch the Sky moved, then again, drawing them over gradually. Bullets and arrows fanned him, a shaft piercing his legging and slicing meat from his inner thigh. As they pounded closer, a brave on a roan surged out ahead of the rest and raised his lance to throw it. Behind Touch the Sky, Sarah fired the big over-and-under. The roan collapsed, crushing the rider.

Big Tree met his eyes across the narrowing distance. Big Tree knew this wily Cheyenne better than most, having been foxed by him several times before. And as he met his eyes, Big Tree suddenly *knew*.

The Comanche war leader's ginger cut suddenly to the right. A few moments later the sky disappeared in a huge spray of dirt and grass. The crack-booming explosion knocked Touch the Sky on his back. Up on the roof, it rained pieces of Comanche and horse all over John Hanchon. When the air cleared, the fight was over.

But Touch the Sky, opening his arms as his sobbing mother rushed into them, watched a lone rider escape to the east. Big Tree would eventually turn north, back to the Sans Arcs and the new combined camp on Wendigo Mountain. The battle was over, yes. But the war had just begun.

"Knobby and Corey will survive," Touch the Sky told Honey Eater, concluding the long narrative of his adventures down in Bighorn Falls. "You should hear them, wife, fighting over whose scar is the finest!"

"Disgraceful," Honey Eater said, keeping the smile from her face only with an effort. "Just as

Indians boast after battle. Perhaps it is the company they keep?"

Touch the Sky grinned. "Perhaps—Corey has taken to copying Two Twists' swaggering walk."

"Little Horse told me about the big medicine up in the Sans Arcs," Honey Eater said, not smiling now. "Although many died, many more were saved, including all the women and children, though some were wounded in their beds."

"Caleb and his miners have a breather now. They seized what explosives were left and returned them to the Army. They may have enough time to fix that track and shore up their defenses. But none of us is safe for long. Not with Big Tree and Sis-ki-dee together on the very edge of our homeland."

"Now," Honey Eater said, voicing his unspoken thought, "when our tribe is unprepared to unify and fight as one. The same mistake that has doomed the entire Red Nation, for tribe wars on tribe while our common enemies destroy us."

She lay in his arms, warm and fragile, fragrant from the fresh columbine braided in her hair. Touch the Sky gently kissed the tissue-thin skin of her eyelids, kissing her eyes shut.

"Not just the two you named," she said. "There is our own Wolf Who Hunts Smiling and Medicine Flute. Do you know what they are preaching lately? They are concentrating on your followers, and they pound a familiar theme: Loyalty to you is disloyalty to the tribe. Or as the eloquent Wolf puts it: 'sentiment has become sedition.' They are determined to drive you out."

Touch the Sky nodded. It was good to be here,

lying close with the most beautiful woman in camp, as safe as it was possible for him to be. This fine and courageous woman was his bride now, and that fact alone justified all his sufferings.

But from here he could glance out the entrance of their tipi and see the distant peak of Wendigo Mountain. Even from here he could not miss the dark storm clouds gathered around the mountain like writhing snakes—symbolic of the great struggle to come against this deadly new Renegade Nation led by his worst tribal enemy.

Touch the Sky reached up and closed the elkskin flap, leaving the two of them in privacy.

"Yes," he whispered to his wife as he slid her soft doeskin dress off to expose even softer skin, "my enemies are determined. But I have more to live for than they. Now never mind the life of the little day, Honey Eater."

And despite the troubles pressing in on the two lovers from all sides, they were soon aware of nothing except the private little world of joy and love they made for themselves.

CHEYENNE GIANT EDITION:

BLOOD ON THE ARROWS

JUDD COLE

Follow the adventures of Touch the Sky, as he searches for a world he can call his own—in a Giant Special Edition!

Born the son of a Cheyenne warrior, raised by frontier settlers, Touch the Sky returns to his tribe and learns the ways of a mighty shaman. Then the young brave's most hated foe is brutally slain, and he stands accused of the crime. If he can't prove his innocence, he'll face the wrath of his entire people—and the hatred of the woman he loves.

_3839-0 $5.99 US/$7.99 CAN

CHEYENNE

JUDD COLE

Follow the adventures of Touch the Sky as he searches for a world he can call his own!

#3: Renegade Justice. When his adopted white parents fall victim to a gang of ruthless outlaws, Touch the Sky swears to save them—even if it means losing the trust he has risked his life to win from the Cheyenne.

___3385-2 $3.50 US/$4.50 CAN

#4: Vision Quest. While seeking a mystical sign from the Great Spirit, Touch the Sky is relentlessly pursued by his enemies. But the young brave will battle any peril that stands between him and the vision of his destiny.

___3411-5 $3.50 US/$4.50 CAN

Jake McMasters

Follow the action-packed adventures of Clay Taggart, as he fights for revenge against settlers, soldiers, and savages.

#5: Bloodbath. Taggart turned the ragtag band of Apache into the fiercest fighters the Southwest has ever seen. They are his army; he uses them to kill his enemies. But on a bloody raid into the stinking wastes of Mexico, some of his men rebel. Far from familiar territory, Taggart has to battle for his life, while trying to reform his warriors into a wolf pack capable of slaughtering anyone who crosses their path.

__3689-4 $3.99 US/$4.99 CAN

#6: Blood Treachery. Settlers, soldiers, and Indians alike have tried to kill the White Apache. But it will take more than brute strength to defeat the wily desperado—it will take cold cunning and ruthless deception. And when a rival chieftain sets out to betray Taggart and his fierce band, they learn that the face of a friend can sometimes hide the heart of an enemy.

__3739-4 $3.99 US/$4.99 CAN